# DIRTY DEALS

## ALAN LEE

Dirty Deals

by Alan Lee

Copyright © 2022 Alan Janney

First Edition
Printed in USA

Cover by eBookLaunch
Formatting by Vellum

Paperback ISBN: 9798849437941

Sparkle Press

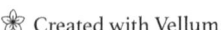 Created with Vellum

~

Stop quoting laws to us.
  We carry swords.
  -Pompey

# 1

A hot July day, me in my office and the central air conditioning doing its best, vacillating between insufficient and arctic. At the moment, the vent was pumping in damp vapors and misting the window, which was necessarily open. If I didn't keep the window open, the A/C moisture accumulated and turned my papers limp. Later in the day, however, the Roanoke humidity would rise and I'd be forced to shut the window, and then freeze, the A/C misting me, and I'd have to flee. A deadly cycle. I was consoled by the notion that Batman had similar drafty issues in the Bat Cave. Me and him, couple of heroes. Something else we had in common, neither of us enjoyed our celebrity.

Mine was a fairly mild celebrity, but thus far it chafed. Articles about me in the paper and magazines had unearthed the crazies, and my inbox overflowed with requests.

My ex-boyfriend stole our cat.

I was abducted by aliens.

My cow can talk.

My parents' house is haunted.

I lost my passport.

My ex-wife is dating someone new.

I want to steal the Declaration of Independence. *Vamanos.*

That last one was from Manny.

Furious that social media was increasing the distance and hatred between tribes in America, he thought most of her historical treasures should be given to him for safe-keeping.

I no longer checked the emails, nor did I listen to voice mails from strangers, nor did I leave my door open. Checking the emails would trigger guilt about not accepting jobs or even replying, so I pretended they didn't exist. Same with calls. The overwhelming tide made me want to do none of it.

The pace of the emails had slackened recently, which was promising. Life would return to normal soon, and in the meantime I would contemplate the ceiling, and my celebrity, and my Nationals World Series hangover.

The wooden stairs leading up to my fortress of solitude politely creaked, and the sliver of light under the locked door darkened. Georgina Princess August turned from her post at the window and padded to the door and sniffed. She turned to look at me and she pleaded.

*Oh please oh please, this one smells friendly. Oh please oh please, I need more people please.*

"No one has knocked," I told her.

*This one would scratch my back and I love that, please oh please.*

A rapping at the door.

Whoever it was, the knock was civil and apologetic, something I admired in intruders.

I took GPA by the collar and unlocked the door, and a nice-looking woman clasped her hands in front of her.

"Good morning. Mr. August?"

"Yes indeed."

"I found the right place. First try," she said.

"It's modest but it's mine."

"You're, ah, broader than I expected." She held out her hands to indicate girth. Each wrist tinkled with expensive-looking bracelets. "The picture looked like this, but you're..." She widened her hands. "Broader than advertised."

"I do not advertise."

"And who is this *angel*?" she said, and she and Georgina Princess fell to it, smiles and affection and panting.

*Oh yes, oh yes, I knew it, I knew it, I am so happy.*

We came into the office and I closed the door and locked it, and the woman didn't mind. She sat in my client chair and ran her hands up and down GPA's neck, making cones with her fingers for the ears.

"Would you like coffee?" I said.

"No thank you. What is her name?"

"Georgina Princess."

"Oh how perfect, how *darling*." She was perhaps fifty-five, in tiptop shape. She wore a seersucker long-sleeve fit-and-flair tunic dress that reached her knees. The dress was embroidered with bold pink, and I'd noticed women wearing too-bright bold colors to alert the world they had money. Her eyes were big and blue, and her hair was dyed a good blonde. With a bankroll and a tan and an adept hairstylist, modern women could wear shorter dresses for longer and look natural doing it, and it was nice for them and nice for me. "I have a teacup Yorkie, a preposterous little devil, but it's all my husband will allow. I miss having a big beautiful animal around. My name is Samantha."

"Mine is Mackenzie."

"Samantha Miller. From Boonsboro."

"Hello Samantha Miller." I received the impression she wanted me to know the names Miller and Boonsboro. A better-bred detective would've, but I was common. "What brings you?"

"You are accepting new clients?"

"For the sake of my dog, I will listen."

"I wish to hire you." She released GPA and clasped her hands on her lap. Perched on the edge of my chair, her ankles tucked demurely beneath, her posture elite, she could be posing for a photo. "Rather, I should say, we wish to hire you."

"Who is we?"

"My Sunday School class. I attend First Baptist. In Boonsboro. Lynchburg, of course."

"Of course," I said.

"Do you know it?"

"I don't, but I like Baptists. Great casseroles."

"You'd adore us, Mr. August. The best casseroles since 1886," she said. "Despite what Rivermont Presbyterian says."

"What about hellfire sermons?"

She smiled and raised her hand to her chin.

"We're up to *here* in hellfire and damnation."

"I might bring my son. His salvation could use a good scare," I said.

"And with Baptists, you get none of the Catholic pedophilia. We're old-fashioned and conservative."

"Do you think Catholics get a bad rap? Maybe the Catholics were just the first to openly deal with their sin. Maybe we should encourage their transparency and progress instead of shame them for it, because we're all glass houses worried about the next brick."

"Oh." Samantha's big blues blinked. "Oh I don't know if I can comment on that, Mr. August."

*Oh I wish, oh how I wish some thoughts you wouldn't share with other persons, oh I wish, because I like her,* said GPA.

"I'm probably wrong. It's happened before. How can I help your Sunday School class?" I said.

"Do you recall a man named Caleb James?"

"I don't. I should, I suppose?"

"I feel dirty saying it. His name, I mean," she said.

"Who is Caleb James?"

"He is the gentleman who escaped from... No, I won't say gentleman. He is the convict who escaped from Wallens Ridge prison earlier this year," she said.

I nodded some understanding.

"You remember the prison break, no doubt," said Samantha.

"I am mortified. But no."

"Are prison breaks not of consequence? I assumed they were, especially in the world of... Well, your world. The law enforcement world."

"Wallens Ridge is three hours west of here. It's of consequence, but a distant one. If he escaped from Roanoke City Jail, five blocks down, I'd be atwitter with it," I said.

"Caleb James is a murderer, Mr. August."

"Still on the lam?"

"Yes. He's at large." She said at large like she was pleased with it.

"Why is a Lynchburg Sunday school class concerned? You are two hundred miles removed from Wallens Ridge Prison."

"Caleb James killed a policeman and maimed another.

Policewoman, I should say. Those two officers? They were from Lynchburg," said Samantha.

Some part of my brain flashed with the memory.

"Shot in the line of duty. One officer died, one lost his hand. Two years ago?" I said.

"It made both CNN and Fox News, though the video of Lynchburg wasn't flattering. Officer Ervin Lane lost his left hand, and Officer Kim Harper lost her life. Shot by Caleb James, the man who escaped from state prison, and he remains *at large*. The good people of Lynchburg were told that he would be recaptured quickly, and yet..." She held up her hands. Sure enough, Caleb James wasn't in them.

"He shot them before Wallens Ridge? Or after?"

Samantha frowned and it made the tiniest of creases in her smooth forehead. "I don't follow your question."

"Was he in Wallens Ridge prison because he shot them? Or did he escape and then shoot them?"

"Oh I see. He shot them and was sent to prison for it. After six months in prison, he escaped. The chief of police has tried everything, he says, but..."

"Which chief?" I said.

"I beg your pardon?"

"The police chief in Pound?"

"Pound, Mr. August? You've lost me."

"Pound, Virginia. I believe that's the town adjacent to Wallens Ridge," I said. "Or is it Big Stone Gap?"

"How unusual. Pound, Virginia," she said. A lesser man would crack jokes. Not I, Mackenzie August, puritan. "The chief I meant is in Lynchburg. Lynchburg's chief of police."

"How is the Lynchburg chief involved in the recapture of a fugitive in Pound, three hours outside his domain?" I said.

"Oh, I see. I understand." She nodded. Graciously. She

did it well, like a mother to her toddler. "Caleb James was spotted in Lynchburg on multiple occasions since, Mr. August. He returned."

"Ah hah."

She smiled. "Yes."

"Any guesses why Caleb returned to Lynchburg?"

"He grew up there. I can't say why he returned, other than that. Our police force hunted everywhere. But..." She held up her hands again.

"How is the First Baptist Sunday School involved?"

"Kim Harper, the poor sweetheart who was shot and killed? Her mother was a long-standing member of our class. A dear friend of mine. Tragically we lost her three years ago. Then her daughter Kim was shot in the line of duty? Horrible for us, as you can imagine. And now, and *now* Mr. August, her killer is at large. Ideally, Lynchburg would handle this itself. We're a proud, independent people. But members of our class were quite taken with the articles written about you, and so here I am."

"You want me to find Caleb James."

"Yes."

"For the emotional well-being of the First Baptist Sunday school class in Boonsboro."

"We'll pay you to do so," she said.

"Your Sunday School class will."

"I brought a check." She slipped it out from a pocket in her dress. "I hope that works. We don't have a credit card."

"Your class has checks?"

"Of course, Mr. August. I can tell you're not Baptist, despite your fondness of us. *Can* you find him? Do you think? Is that something private detectives do? It would mean so much to those who cherished Kim Harper."

"If he's on the run, Ms. Miller, for—"

"*Mrs.* Miller," she said.

"If Caleb has been running for months, Mrs. Miller, I cannot guarantee anything. He could be in New Zealand in a hobbit hole."

"Or he could still be in Lynchburg, his hometown."

"If he's a fool," I said.

"When he shot the officers, he was high on crystal methamphetamine. He's a fool, Mr. August." She placed the check on my desk. It was blank.

I loved those.

"And besides." Samantha held out her hands again and GPA leapt into her grasp, and she bent over him. "You'll bring this beautiful beautiful girl, and she'll find him! Yes she will. *Yes* she will."

"Yesterday I threw a tennis ball at Georgina. The ball hit her between the eyes, rolled under a dining room chair, and despite her best efforts she couldn't locate it," I said.

"One of you two will find Caleb, I'm sure. After all, the Lord is on our side."

"That's comforting."

"I wasn't making a joke, Mr. August."

"Nor was I, Mrs. Miller."

Her head raised up from the dog. She glanced to see if I was looking down her dress—the neckline had draped open. I wasn't, and she saw I wasn't, and she looked pleased. A scrupulous man, I might make a Baptist after all.

"Good," she said. "You will take the case? Is that how it's said?"

"I'll start tomorrow and give you a week. By then, I'll know if finding Caleb James is feasible, and we'll discuss it further."

"Might you not find him within that week?" she said.

I shrugged. I did it with as much modesty as I had. Like a rich Baptist from Boonsboro would.

"If anyone could."

"Terrific, Mr. August. That's *terrific*."

GPA thought so too.

## 2

Ronnie had a friend over. A girl she'd gone to Franklin County High School with as teenagers. They'd danced on the same competitive team. Now they drank white wine in my living room and watched their two boys play.

Ronnie still looked like a dancer. Her fitness was apparent, especially when she sat and crossed her legs, and you realized her stomach and thighs met at a strong angle with no stomach overhang. The same way Manny's did. The same way mine did not.

Her friend Charlotte Andrews looked like most former dancers did in their thirties. Some of the grace and poise remained, if the flexibility and musculature did not. Charlotte's hair was dark and chin length and she had bangs. I *know,* bangs. But they worked for her, and the complete picture was of a woman who'd gone into adulthood without a plan, had partied hard in her twenties, had gotten by on her looks, and now she was a mom and a little lost in the world.

Also, she'd had rhinoplasty.

"I cannot get over," said Charlotte, "how gorgeous you are."

"And I cannot get over," said Ronnie, "you marrying Willy Pierce. Willy Wonka Pierce."

"He was only my starter husband. We barely slept under the same roof. I was always off doing... You know, doing things I couldn't tell my husband about. I think he's designing windows at Ply Gem." Charlotte raised her glass of wine. "Here's to setting my twenties on fire."

"My thirties are a dream, by comparison," said Ronnie.

"Veronica Summers, in her thirties. Who would've thought she'd get even *more* hot." Charlotte laughed and Ronnie did too. Kix glared at Charlotte's son. "Or that Veronica Summers could clean a house so well."

"Oh, this isn't me. The men who live here clean. I married him for his body, his heart, and his sponge."

"And he cooks, too?" said Charlotte.

"He loves it. He makes me wish I could. Sometimes I worry that women's empowerment cost us our imagination. Do you think? We're letting men have all the fun."

I was in the kitchen cooking duck à l'orange.

It was not fun.

I'd purchased two plucked and gutted ducks to make the recipe simpler, thinking surely a man's man could handle this. A colossal and aspirational lapse in judgment. I'd been roasting the ducks and simmering carrots, tomatoes, celery, hearts, and gizzards for an hour. I added the stock and wine, and now I watched the sauce with trepidation as I cut the orange zest into a julienne. Soon I'd need to boil the sugar and vinegar into a syrup, and then do something with orange juice and jelly, but I'd forgotten what.

"Mackenzie, do you have a brother? God, I'd marry a man who cooks and cleans," said Charlotte.

"I do not cook and clean. I live well," I said.

I wiped my forehead with the back of the hand holding a knife. Never let them see you sweat.

"What's the difference?"

"It's heaven all the way to heaven, Charlotte," I said.

"What?"

"He's quoting someone," said Ronnie. "I never know who."

"You should've seen Ron in high school, Mackenzie. She would walk through campus and the boys would chase her, too afraid to speak, hoping she'd drop something they could pick up. Her dad wouldn't let her out much, but when he did... Ron, remember the dock parties at Waters Edge? *Gawd*," said Charlotte.

Kix teetered into the kitchen.

*Father*, he said. *Here's the thing. Friendship is overrated.*

I handed him a slice of orange.

*This doesn't help.*

"Go play," I said.

*Look*, he said. *Just look, please, at that dishonest, stinking, foul, unpleasant malcontent. He took my car, you know.*

On the rug, sitting between Charlotte's ankles—which were still good—a boy was chewing on a toy truck. Not much intelligence shined in his eyes.

"Do your best."

*I will not, and I'm considering*, he said, *a tantrum.*

Charlotte was in our living room because she was under-taking her second divorce, and Ronnie did those. Her second husband was a few years older and going through the pain of a renaissance that often came in our forties. He'd sold his two restaurants and was working on the great American novel, and Charlotte couldn't bear it.

"I married a man of purpose," she said. "Not a beatnik."

"It sounds like his career transition has been hard on you," said Ronnie.

"On both of us." Charlotte indicated her kid with the glass of wine. "It's quite taxing."

"Having his father around has been difficult on Ethan?"

"Oh yes. His schedule is entirely disrupted, Ron. He's a brilliant baby, brilliant, but since his father quit... He just *quit*. And now Ethan can't make heads or tails."

Ethan, by the look of it, was crapping his pants.

Kix sat hard on his butt in the kitchen and glared some more, and when I tried to return him to the living room he whimpered and fussed, and Ronnie said to let him be, so I did. Instead I strained the sauce and set it to a simmer while I hunted for the Grand Marnier, and Ronnie explained the next stages of divorce proceedings to Charlotte.

Ten minutes passed and the nostalgia wore off for Ronnie, and I was pouring the fat out of the ducks' roasting pan, and Charlotte finally realized her kid needed to be refreshed.

"Mackenzie doesn't change diapers, does he," said Charlotte. She laughed. Ronnie did not.

She stood. "Charlotte, I'm so glad you came by. I'll email you soon."

"Okay, okay. I get the hint. I'll go." Charlotte laughed again.

Ronnie smiled.

I rotated the ducks and turned them breast side up.

*That kid stinks*, said Kix. *I realize there's some hypocrisy here, but when I do it it's adorable. Right?*

"Would you like to change him upstairs before you go?" said Ronnie.

"No, that's okay, Ron, I'll do it in the car."

Ronnie opened the door for Charlotte, who was holding her kid like a football and shouldering her purse.

"Before you go, keep in mind—it's cheaper to keep her," said Ronnie.

"Beg your pardon?"

"It's a saying that means divorce often solves very little. And it costs a fortune."

"Maybe you'll give me the Franklin County Eagle *discount*?" She laughed again.

"So good to see you again, Charlotte."

"You *too*, Ron!"

Ronnie closed the door after her. "I need more wine."

*Me too*, said Kix.

"I hate ducks," I said.

Ronnie hugged me from behind, something she knew I liked, for reasons that are obvious, and she said, "Can I pour you a glass?"

I would've enjoyed her breath on my ear if I hadn't been warm already.

"A cold beer, please," I said.

She cracked a can of Devil's Backbone and poured it into a frosty mug and she sat on the other side of the counter from me.

"Mackenzie."

"Yes Ronnie."

"Charlotte," she said.

"Yeah."

"She was more fun in high school."

"Or maybe your standards were lower." I set the timer on the oven—another forty minutes, preposterous—and wiped my hands and picked up the beer. "Here's looking at you, kid."

"That's from *Casablanca*?"

"I wonder how much of myself originates in Rick Blaine? The modern independent man," I said.

"You're both tough. Hard on the outside, soft on the inside. Good with one-liners."

"We both hate the Nazis and have a thing for blondes."

"I'm not naturally blonde," she said.

"That's a shame. We'll always have Paris."

She sipped her wine. "Did you listen to Charlotte?"

"I did my best to ignore her. And I failed."

"She's the first divorce case I've had since I married you," she said.

"And?"

"It looks different now, divorce. It's no longer a termination of a legal contract. It's... It's somehow more important than the law. It's bigger."

"A holy thing. Not to be easily cast aside?" I said.

"I wonder if I should tell her that."

"If it's more important than the law, and you're a lawyer, maybe so."

"I'm not a marriage counselor, though," she said.

"I'm no chef. But I'm doing my best."

The corners of her mouth curled and her lips peaked in a smile. "Have the ducks defeated you?"

I cracked the oven and peered in.

"Still to be determined. But we may be ordering takeout."

"Smells divine. Who else is eating?"

"Only us tonight. Me and my damn good-looking woman," I said.

"Duck à l'orange for little ol' me, Mackenzie?"

"I always cook for an audience of one. Also, phooey. I forgot the butter." I took two sticks from the refrigerator.

"An intimate dinner. I love those."

"And perhaps an edible one."

"I believe I'll change." Ronnie turned the television to Sesame Street, and she moved for the stairs.

"You already look great."

"If it's only us, Mackenzie," she said. "I'll be wearing a slutty dress."

"I love those."

"I know."

"If you insist."

"I do. That way, no matter how we fare with the duck, we'll have dessert." She winked and disappeared upstairs.

"Might be an early bedtime," I told Kix, who'd wandered toward the television. "You know, if Charlotte said things like that, about slutty dresses, to her husband, they might be—"

*Shhhh*, shouted Kix. *You're interrupting Elmo, which I cannot abide.*

"Sorry."

*And besides, fixing marriage isn't that simple.*

He had a point.

# 3

Lynchburg, Virginia was a stubborn city.

John Lynch had settled it in 1757, primarily as a ferry service for crossing the James River. When the river proved too difficult, the town pivoted to tobacco and prospered. In 1850, Virginia's general assembly wouldn't fund construction of a railway line to the town, so the citizens funded it themselves, and prospered. During the Civil War, Lynchburg was the only city not recaptured by the Union, refusing to surrender until days after the war was over. The town survived the Great Depression with factories that supported both world wars. Recently, Liberty University's explosion helped Lynchburg weather a sharp decline in population. Instead of receding as factories closed, Lynchburg bloomed into a college town. Now it was one of the largest cities I'd ever been to that had no interstate connection—it was reached by backroads and small highways only. Built onto the side of a large hill, the downtown region fought gravity every day. Time had tried to forget it, but Lynchburg kept finding new ways to thrive. Proud and stubborn and unimpressed with me when I arrived in my Honda Accord.

It had been a leisurely seventy-five minute drive from Roanoke through Bedford farm country, and I arrived on Court Street at 9:30 a.m. The narrow lane was crowded with a police station, the US Marshal's office, law offices, and *three* courthouses, all perched on Court Street at the top of the steep hillside of Lynchburg.

I'd made an appointment with Terrance Goodwin, the Commonwealth's Attorney who handled Caleb James' case. He met me on the district courthouse steps and shook my hand. Despite the heat, Terrance wore a thin argyle vest over his button-down shirt. Plus a bowtie and wireless glasses. His brown suede shoes were Nike Air Force Ones, and I bet the judges he worked with had never noticed.

The courthouse was a hundred years old and they'd done their best with modern carpet, but the walls were still plaster and the floors creaked hollowly in places. His desk was wooden, solid and well-constructed and ancient, and had belonged to whomever had the office before him, and probably the person before that.

Terrance was a Black man, fit, with a shaved head, and according to the photo on his wall he'd married a White woman with a shaved head. The kid they posed with had the longest hair in the family.

"Samantha Miller hired you," he said.

"You know her."

"Everyone knows Samantha Miller. She's gentry, so to speak."

"She'd be tickled pink to hear it," I said. "Technically, her Sunday School class is my client."

"I coulda guessed. Civil warfare out in Boonsboro. The Baptists and the Presbyterians and the Episcopalians. Nice folk, but they dearly love to outshine the other." He laced his fingers behind his head.

"And Caleb James was…"

"Presbyterian, right off Rivermont, which might as well be Camelot. I heard his parents had to quit attending. Samantha's already gone around town, I'm sure, making sure it's known the Baptists are on the case, won't rest until the wayward Presbyterian is behind bars again where he belongs."

"And by extension, all of them," I said.

"My man. Got that right."

"Where do you stand? Biblically speaking."

"I attend Thomas Road Baptist Church," he said. "On Liberty University's campus."

"Jerry Falwell's old place. You're Baptist too."

"Biggest church in town, but the old guard won't recognize us. We're Baptists by convenience, vagrants, merely passing through." He grinned. "Drives them crazy, all the press we get."

"Pharisees, the lot of them."

"White-washed tombs. Heavy on the white. But you probably aren't here to rap about denominations."

"Caleb James. You prosecuted the case," I said.

Terrance nodded.

"It went down my first week on the job. I didn't know the involved parties, so I became the so-called special prosecutor."

"Lucky you."

"Trial by fire," he said. "We made one news cycle on the twenty-four-hour cable channels. And now you're gonna catch him."

"I don't know much about Caleb. I'll take anything you got."

He pursed his lip and looked thoughtfully through me a moment.

"Judge Ward gagged us. Even though the case's closed, I still tread lightly on it.

"Spill as much tea as you can," I said. "Then I'll go find other teapots."

Gears were turning between his ears, him thinking through what was common knowledge. His reluctance was stimulating, because it meant much was still hidden.

"Caleb James grew up here. Came from some money, his father was a dentist. Nice kid, I'm told. Athlete, played baseball. He was one of the valedictorians at Virginia Episcopal." He chuckled, and it was an open, friendly sound. "Even the Presbyterians send their kids there. Caleb went to UVA for finance, and then got an internship on Wall Street. One of those coveted stock trading jobs you see movies about? He wasn't offered a full-time position when his internship ended, and the story goes he was suspected of skimming profits, though nothing was proven, and I didn't feel like investigating it. Like I said, I was new. Anyway, he returned home to open an investment office. But..." He sucked at his teeth like one does when the story takes a sharp turn. "He'd picked up a cocaine habit in the big city. According to him, he couldn't find enough coke down here so he switched to meth. He was flying high when Officers Lane and Harper pulled him over."

"Were Lane and Harper local?" I said.

"Yep, though Kim went off to college in Richmond. She returned for the job. Ervin Lane never left."

"Ervin Lane lost his hand."

"He did."

"Does he still live nearby?"

Terrance twisted in his chair. "I don't know."

That felt, I thought, dishonest. I stored it for later use.

"I stopped for gas on the way here and read a WSET

article reviewing the charges, but details were scarce about that traffic stop," I said.

"Gag order. Details are still scarce."

"What happened?"

"Caleb James was high. Stumbled out of the car and resisted arrest. He pulled a gun and shot them both. Ervin's hand was half blown off but he wrestled the gun away and called for backup," said Terrance.

"With one hand, Ervin outwrestled a guy high on meth?"

"Sure did."

"Did Caleb run? How did Ervin..." I held out my hands, searching for words. "How did he do anything? He'd hand was shot off."

"Not completely off. Half off. It was hanging on," said Terrance.

"You're disgusting, sir."

He shrugged. "How it went down. Anyway, Ervin had a couple inches and fifty pounds on Caleb. That's part of it."

"Was there a dashcam?" I said.

"Yes, but the struggle took place off camera. No help there. All you can see is Officer Harper get shot."

"That's hard to watch."

"God-awful," said Terrance.

"Can I watch the video?"

"You could ask Judge Ward. And after he's done paddling you, he'll tell you voyeurs should go to hell and to get out of his city."

"I like him. He sounds Baptist," I said.

"One of the oldest battle-ax Baptists."

"Did Caleb run?"

"You know, Mr. August, I probably already said too much about that night. Not much more from me there. Caleb was arrested. Went through withdrawals in jail. Nasty guy, attacked one of the deputies a few weeks in. Pled guilty for a reduced sentence. Got thirty years, and that was the end of my involvement. For the rest of the story, you'll need another source."

"The article stated he was hit with second degree murder."

"He was," said Terrance.

"Killing an officer in the line of duty, and maiming another, that's capital murder easy."

"He pled it down," said Terrance.

"You're lucky the news vans were gone by then, him not getting capital."

Another chuckle. Less friendly. That was the only response.

I said, "Why a plea deal at all? Or if so, why not first degree?"

"Detective." Terrance was making some hard and direct eye contact. We'd wandered into a mine field. Sometimes us detectives are pains in the rear. "The man was high. There was a fight. He claimed he didn't mean to do it. In fact, he claimed innocence. The town was in an uproar, a real circus. Judge Ward didn't want a trial, he wanted Caleb remanded to a federal penitentiary yesterday. So we cut a deal. I consulted Officer Lane about the deal before signing it, and he approved, and Ward sent Caleb James away for thirty years without possibility of parole. Thirty years is thirty years. Justice was served and Lynchburg could grieve and move on."

"Caleb claimed innocence?"

"Initially. But don't forget, he was flying high that night."

"What'd he say happened?" I said.

"He didn't remember, that's part of it. Tell you what, Detective. If you find him, ask him. Then haul him back to prison. The man's still got twenty-eight to go." Terrance smiled with some politeness. But it was a *Now get the hell out* smile.

"We're done, aren't we," I said.

"I'm done. Unless you want to talk the Lynchburg Hellcat baseball team."

"They're awful."

"They are. Still, a couple prospects on their way to the majors. Do you watch the Salem Sox?" said Terrance.

"Next time Hellcats are in town, I'll buy you a dog and a beer."

He said, "I'll take you up on that," but he didn't mean it.

I stood and nodded toward the window. "I heard Caleb was spotted back in town."

"I heard that too."

"Did you hear why? I'm searching for leads."

Terrance stood too and he shrugged, and stuck his hands in his pockets.

"You don't just quit crystal meth," he said.

**4**

---

I strolled the hill to the US Marshal's office. In all likelihood, the marshals would find Caleb James before I did. They weren't chumps.

I was no chump either. But I was outnumbered.

It wasn't like entering a dentist's—there was no receptionist. There was a metal door and a phone, and nothing else. Not even a chair. I bet their Yelp reviews weren't encouraging. I picked up the phone and it rang immediately and a woman answered.

"Lynchburg Marshal's Office."

"Justice. Integrity. Service. And no chairs," I said.

"Come again, sir?"

"Your motto. Justice. Integrity. Service. Did you know that?"

"I did. Do you have an appointment?"

"I don't," I said.

"How can I help?"

Two cameras watched the room. One above the metal door, one above the phone. I withdrew my wallet and I badged the phone camera. "I'm looking for Caleb James, the escapee. I wonder if I could compare notes with your fugitive crew."

"I can't see the badge well, sir. What's your affiliation?" she said.

"Roanoke private detective. Hired by Lynchburg aristocracy to find the escapee."

"*Oh*," said the phone. "Are you the gentleman sleuth we read about? The train caught in the avalanche?"

Mackenzie August. Massively in vogue.

"It was a blizzard," I said, "not an avalanche. Do you think the article made me sound too good to be true? I worry it did."

"And you're on the Caleb James manhunt now? How about that, a local celebrity. What was your name again? I forgot."

"Mackenzie August."

"That's *it*, Mackenzie August," she said.

I nodded some encouragement.

"Mackenzie, our deputies are either at the courthouse or jail at the moment. We only have four, we're a small office."

"I'll leave my card with the phone, in case they show an interest in cooperation."

"To be honest, Mackenzie, I don't know that our deputies will," she said.

"Does it help if I'm friends with Deputy Martinez?"

"Oh my *Lord* yes. Do you work with Manny?"

"He works with *me*. And I recently beat him at the bench press," I said.

"I just love that man."

"*Manny es un bebé grande.*"

"You said it!" She laughed. "I'll make a note. Come back with Deputy Martinez and I'll buzz you right in."

I slid my card out of my wallet and waved it at her, and set it on top of the phone's wall housing.

"Tell Manny Inglath says hello!" She made a noise like a high-pitched laugh and I hung up, irked Manny opened doors I couldn't.

I left and climbed up the hill to the police station—seriously, they were all in a line—and spoke with the front desk officer, a cop who'd gained so much weight his only remaining function was to sit at a table. He wouldn't let a private cop from Roanoke speak to the chief, but I mentioned Caleb James and he said, "Hang on a sec," and he waddled deeper into the office and returned six minutes later. "Come on back, he finally hung up."

Police Chief Jake Robertson stood at his desk, staring at the papers on it. He was a short guy, maybe five feet-six inches, and his head was shaved, and he was built like a prize fighter. Thick fingers, beefy hands, forearms like a ham. His office was sweltering and sweat ran down his scalp.

"You're a private cop out of Roanoke?" he said in a bright bark.

"Mackenzie August."

"Jake Robertson." We shook hands. Mine were bigger, his might've been harder. "I'm busy as hell, but I hear you're looking for that son of a bitch Caleb James. Tell you what, you find him before the marshals, do us all a favor and put that boy down."

"He's public enemy number one," I said. "Got any leads?"

He pivoted at the waist, far enough to smack the plaster wall behind him, and the glossy mugshot pinned there. The mugshot was of a thin guy, baggy eyes, hollow cheeks, looked like hell if hell had a rough night.

"That's Caleb. He showed up here three days after he got

loose. I don't know how he did that, by the way, and last I heard Big Stone Gap didn't either. He showed up and you know the first thing he did? Well... Maybe I won't tell you that, not sure it's common knowledge. But the second thing he did? He went straight to his dealer. That ol' boy drove directly to his meth dealer. Once a junkie always a junkie. We heard after the fact, and his dealer don't know where he went, lowlife named Marky. You can go rough him up too, Marky, lives off Stable Avenue, the only trailer on it. But no, I don't have any solid leads and if the marshals do they haven't told me. They know I'd go find him and handle it myself and bury his body, that skinny bastard. He shot Kim Harper and took the hand of Ervin Lane, my best detective."

I wanted to pressure the chief on the thing that wasn't common knowledge, but I thought I could get it from someone else, and stay on the chief's good side by not asking. It sounded like a clue and I loved those.

"Ervin was a detective?" I said.

"'Scuse me, not a detective, a patrolman. He was my best patrolman too," said Chief Robertson. His hands were holding onto his belt and his eyes were everywhere, an excess of angry energy. I got the feeling he grew up on a farm, work to be done all the time, hard hands built organically, and maybe he still went home to tend his chickens and goats and not waste time on slow conversation.

"*Was*? Ervin retired?"

"He did. We tried everything to keep Ervin. You know, find work he could do with a prosthetic? Lost his hand at the wrist. He could man the emergency lines, he could drive prisoner transport, he could work the front desk... He was our best man, heart and soul of the office, but he never recovered from the loss, not really. He medically retired and moved away, about six months ago."

"Caleb James escaped six months ago. Is that a coinci-dence?" I said.

Robertson straightened his back, like stretching. "You'd have to ask Ervin. Actually, check that. No, don't ask him. I'd prefer you leave Ervin alone. Man's been through enough."

"Where'd he move?"

"Out of the state and that's all I'll tell you," said Robertson.

"It's a secret."

"Okay, listen, I'll tell you something. It's not common knowledge but I'll tell you anyway, so's we're on the same team, here. Caleb James escaped and you know where he went first?"

"His old meth dealer."

"Before that. He drove to Ervin Lane's house. You know what he did? He burned it down. Three days after Caleb escaped, and poor Ervin Lane's house is torched to the ground. Fuckin' Caleb James tried to kill him. Fortunately Ervin wasn't there. Means, now, James is on the loose with a mind to kill Ervin, and no I'm not telling a soul where he is."

The chief had answers and I was agog for them. I was hoping he'd sit and get talkative but he hadn't and he wasn't offering.

"Why would Caleb James burn down Ervin Lane's house?" I said.

"Cause James is a got'damn lunatic cop-killing junkie. Maybe he blames Ervin, hell, I don't know. You find him, you ask him, and then you kill him. Hear?" Robertson's voice had risen to a shout and blue veins were visible down the sides of his bald head. "You kill him and don't tell the marshals but you come tell me and I'll buy you a bottle of bourbon and we'll drink to it, and that'll be that."

"Could you ask Ervin Lane if he'll talk to me?" I said. "Over the phone."

"I might ask. I probably won't, though. He doesn't know where Caleb is. And I'd appreciate it if you left poor Ervin alone. And don't go bothering Kim Harper's parents, leave them out of this." Robertson raised his wrist to look at his watch and he said, "Shit."

"Did it bother you that Caleb didn't get capital murder?"

"Hell yeah it bothered me. Bothered all of us, but I eventually signed off on it. Not that they needed me to. Caleb was going to fight us all the way, so we had to twist his arm and get him to plea. Now listen, I got to haul ass. You want a place to start, go rattle his meth dealer, Marky out on Stable. Knock him around and tell him it was from me. You're a big guy, look like you can handle that."

I pointed at the photo of Caleb James.

"A copy of that would be good."

"Absolutely, ask my man at the front, and good luck to you," said Robertson and then he was gone, moving double-time down the hall. A distant door boomed.

I walked to the front and the fat officer there said, "I heard, I heard. I'll get you a copy." He stood like he didn't want to.

"I'll take any photos you have. Especially ones where Caleb doesn't look like a corpse, because he probably docsn't normally."

"Sure," said the guy.

"Were you close with Detective Lane?"

"Ervin?" he shouted from the file room. "Sure, I guess. He wasn't a detective, though. He was a patrolman."

On old trick. Get one of the facts wrong, see what happens.

"The chief called Ervin a detective," I said.

"Well..."

The guy returned with a manila folder and he opened it. Inside were photos of Caleb James, not only the mugshot. I was expecting digital copies, but this worked. He slid me a few. Caleb was thin in all of them, even the professional shot from his investing website.

"Why'd the chief call Ervin a detective?" I said.

"Chief got confused, is all. This enough?"

I took three of the photos. "Perfect. Thanks. Ervin get busted down from a detective?"

"Maybe you should mind your own business, Roanoke. We been through a lot here," said the guy and he walked deeper into the police office and I didn't think he was returning until I left. Which was, I thought, hurtful.

## 5

I vacated downtown Lynchburg and drove north through Boonsboro, home to the county's money. And Samantha Miller. By design, Boonsboro had no new construction. The goal was to own one of the grand, centuries-old estates. Only so many existed, inherited through generations, and to own property there meant you mattered. New construction would be sneered at. Politely.

I found Marky's trailer in a seedy park, well away from the money, on Timberlake off Stable, and I banged on the front door and back door, but he wasn't home. A mutt inside barked at me until I left.

One could circle Lynchburg in a neat loop on Rivermont Avenue, west on Boonsboro Road, south on Memorial, east on Lynchburg Expressway, north on Church, and back to Rivermont, merging smoothly through the suburbs, the rural fields, the poorer neighborhoods, and the quaint downtown, almost without stopping. The circuit lasted an hour and I did it twice, listening to old news reports on Caleb James and absorbing his environs.

The thing was, I'd never hunted a wily fugitive. I could

follow a runaway spouse because they were often terrible at it, or they wanted to be found. I could find a persnickety teenager, trying to hide. I knew how to poke around for clues, I knew how to pester people into mistakes. But find a skilled criminal hiding in Arizona or Alaska or Alabama? Doubtful. The combined might of the marshals hadn't found him, so what chance did I have?

Only a puncher's chance.

An obdurate puncher.

Finding his trail in Lynchburg was paramount.

Much of what I heard confused me. Much of what I hadn't heard, too, and I needed to let it settle, ergo I kept lapping the town before driving home.

I plucked Kix from his Montessori school and we met Ronnie at El Mezcal. We ate outside in the shade of an umbrella at a cast iron table, near a babbling water fountain. Ronnie's high heels made clicks on the flagstones, and she walked with bravura and purpose, a talent that men were trained to recognize audibly, and many women too. Those who looked for the source of the sensual clicking saw her and were rewarded by it.

Her skirts had lengthened since we married. Whereas they used to look like she wore a scarf circling her thighs, now the skirt could be a small towel. Still far shorter than any other attorney in town, still minuscule enough that the judges thought it inappropriate but were too enamored to mention it, they stopped above her knee, enough so you could see muscle in her quads and hamstrings, which probably was the point.

I ordered a margarita and she had wine, and Kix asked for tequila but got juice. Kix and I ate chips, and Ronnie abstained, excess carbs her mortal enemy.

Ronnie clinked my class with hers. "To us."

"For always."

"Tell me about the interviews," she said.

"They didn't last long. No one wants to talk about Caleb James. Not the prosecutor, not the police chief, not the marshals."

"They didn't want to discuss *him*? Or they didn't want to remember that night? Or they didn't like the case?" she said. "Or something else?"

"All of the above, perhaps. Some of the facts don't fit. There are gaps in the story, and I don't know why."

Ronnie drank wine and set her glass down. She leaned back in her chair and tilted her face upward toward the sun, beyond the umbrella's shadow. Beneath the table, her toe slipped under my pant leg.

"Tell me. I enjoy listening to a crime story without having to broker its ending."

"Caleb James and Ervin Lane both grew up in Lynchburg. Caleb goes to UVA for finance, and on to Wall Street after. Ervin becomes a cop. Caleb returns to town with a sullied reputation and a coke habit, which morphs into a meth addition. Ervin pulls Caleb over one night, and Caleb is high. Off camera, Caleb pulls a gun and kills Kim Harper, Ervin's partner, and he shoots Ervin too. Ervin loses his hand, but manages to subdue Caleb." I removed a photo of Caleb and set it on the table. Even Kix thought Caleb looks like a corpse. "Caleb pleads innocent, though his story doesn't add up. While in jail, Caleb assaults one of his jailers. The judge wants him gone immediately, and he gags all parties. The prosecutor cuts a deal with Caleb to avoid a trial. Second degree for thirty years, instead of capital murder. Case closed. Caleb is remanded to Wallens Ridge supermax prison in Big Stone Gap. He escapes after two years, which is hard to do. He returns to Lynchburg, and the first thing he does is burn down Ervin Lane's house, but Ervin wasn't home. Around this time, Ervin finally accepts medical retirement and he moves away. Caleb also visits his former meth dealer, and then he vanishes. Which is also hard to do. Marshals can't find him, and so I'm hired to help, but no one wants to talk to me. The end."

"Caleb sounds like a real bitch," said Ronnie.

*Caleb*, said Kix, pondering the chip in his grubby fingers, *is a real bitch.*

Ronnie bit her lip.

I knew better than to reward the language with a reaction, so I stayed cool.

"Wonder where he gets his vocabulary."

"I'm trying to stop," said Ronnie.

*Please don't. The girls think my colorful metaphors make me dangerous and edgy.*

"The best part of your story," said Ronnie, "was listening to your voice. Was Kim Harper born in Lynchburg?"

"Yes."

"Did Caleb and Ervin know one another growing up?"

"That's one of the questions," I said, "to which I need an answer."

"Another is, what leverage did Caleb have to force the plea deal? Second degree for murdering an officer in the line of duty is... startling at best, and a miscarriage of justice at worst. Caleb had something that caused the gag and the reduced charge," she said.

"Agree. Preliminary guess is, Kim Harper or Ervin Lane botched the arrest. Maybe they were too rough with him, or the disaster could've been avoided if they were careful, or something like that."

"What are the other questions you have?"

"Why can't I watch the dashcam? Did Internal Affairs get

involved? Is there a chance Ervin Lane used to be a detective? Why would Caleb risk burning Ervin Lane's house down? Why can't I talk to Ervin?"

*Son of a bitch.*

Instead of smiling at Kix, Ronnie smiled at the sky. "Where'd Ervin go?"

"Ervin retired and moved away, and the police chief won't tell me where. Nor let me talk to him. Ervin probably has PTSD now. Maybe a drinking problem, or worse."

The waiter brought us plates of food. I shared my rice and chicken and peppers with Kix and he longingly gazed at my margarita. So I split it with him. Just kidding, I did not.

"You were hired to find Caleb. Not look into his criminal case," said Ronnie.

"I know."

"Are you being nosey out of habit?"

"I have to start somewhere. Caleb returning and burning down the house of the officer who arrested him seems significant. Someone knows where Caleb is hiding, even if they don't know they know," I said.

Ronnie had sat up and she pushed her fajitas around the hotplate with a fork. "I'm glad you don't make traffic stops, Mackenzie."

"It's a tough job."

"Some stories don't have a happy ending, do they," said Ronnie.

"A meth addict kills one cop and disables another? No happy ending in sight."

"What will you do tomorrow?"

"Talk with Caleb's attorney. I left a message. Haven't heard back. Maybe work up the courage to pester Caleb's parents," I said.

The waiter hurried by and Kix shouted for a margarita and the waiter said, "*Ese es un chico lindo.*"

Kix frowned.

*Those aren't real words. Those are fake Manny words.*

We ate food quietly for a time.

I said, "Would Caleb's lawyer be disinclined to help track her former client, now at large?"

"Probably." Ronnie nodded. "Defense attorneys instinctively protect their client, even after the retainer's gone."

"Rats," I said.

She smiled.

"We're the worst."

"You're not the worst," I said.

"You're biased because I throw myself naked on your bed every chance I get."

I raised my margarita and clinked her glass.

"It's either the tequila talking or you make a good point."

*Gross*, said Kix.

## 6

The next morning over coffee, I scrolled Kim Harper's social media accounts. Two years since she died, but the accounts remained in existence. She'd been cute. Short girl, long brown hair, played softball in her free time, dated a guy from Richmond, where she'd gone to college.

Ervin Lane had no social media, but I found photos. A man heavy with muscle and grist, like a lot of small-town cops. He'd gone prematurely bald and his goatee was more gray than brown, even for a guy in his mid-thirties. He had tattoos on his neck and forearms. Was I the type of detective who stereotyped, I'd say he drank Coors Light and attended NASCAR races and claimed Dale Earnhardt was the best stock-car racer who ever lived.

And he'd be right, I don't care what anyone said about Jeff Gordon or Jimmie Johnson.

Ervin Lane and Kim Harper made an odd couple in the patrol car. Cute college girl, ugly country boy.

Caleb James' social media accounts had been taken down, probably due to harassment. Privileged White guy does drugs and kills a public servant, he was gonna catch hell from the online mob.

I wanted to see Caleb before the cocaine habit. I scrolled three pages of Google results before finding images that weren't his mugshots or trial photographs. At one point he'd been a good-looking guy. Tall, broad shoulders, like the baseball player Terrance Goodwin said he was. In college he'd filled out, maybe two hundred pounds, but Wall Street and meth had taken their toll—he looked one-forty max in his mugshot. Sunken and malnourished.

No wonder Ervin had subdued Caleb with one hand; Ervin had seventy-pounds on him. Terrance guessed fifty but the disparity was greater than that.

I couldn't find birthdays online, but they looked the same age.

"I bet they knew each other," I told the kitchen. That night when Ervin told Caleb to get out of the car, they weren't two strangers staring at each other. There was history.

Bad history?

Enough to make Caleb want to kill Ervin? Enough to make Caleb break out of jail and drive to Ervin's house and burn it down?

What the hell happened that night.

LIKE EVERYONE ELSE, defense attorney Elaine Terry kept her office on Court Street. She had half the lower floor of what once had once been a craftsman house, now a covey of law offices. Terry & Graham Law Firm. Graham had the other half. A different firm was located on the second floor, but I didn't care about them—I was here for Terry. She hadn't returned my call so I walked into her office, which felt like walking through the front door of someone's home from their porch.

To my right, a wide staircase led upward. To my left, a restroom and kitchen. Directly ahead, a desk with a smiling woman. Behind her, the offices of Terry and Graham.

The smiling woman didn't stop smiling but she stood and said, "Oh dear. You're Mr. August."

"You didn't wonder if I was Robert Redford?"

She came around her desk and took my hand. It was kind of a handshake, and kind of a squeeze, like you'd give a friend when their dog died. She wore a flowery dress, the kind I pictured Marilla Cuthbert wore to church in Green Gables with Anne. Her face was warm and round.

She enjoyed baking. She had to. I could smell bread coming out of the oven.

"I passed on both your messages, Mr. August, I did." She squeezed again. "She's been busy, so very busy, but between you and me, Mr. August, I don't know that she has a mind to discuss Caleb James."

"You must be her paralegal," I said. "And guardian angel."

She hadn't stopped smiling, but it was a commiserating, guilty smile. "I am, I am, I'm her office assistant too. She and Jason Graham share me, so to speak. But she's not in right now, Mr. August. Ms. Terry's representing the mother in a nasty custody hearing down the street, just awful."

"How'd you know who I am?"

She laughed and patted my arm with one hand, the other still holding onto my fingers. She wasn't old enough to be a grandmother, but I bet she was a favorite aunt.

"Well, I looked you up, didn't I? We heard about the handsome gentleman going up and down the street and asking questions. It's a small community, you know. Only one street and windows everywhere. I got the call immediately, and of course we all heard what Samantha Miller did, hiring you. Small town, big mouths, haha."

I nodded. I grinned. I gave her *aw shucks*.

A talkative paralegal was like Mike Tyson's left hook—a sneaky way to get everything.

I looked over her shoulder at her desk.

Mrs. Gardner.

"Mrs. Gardner—"

"Sally." Another squeeze.

"Sally, did you know Caleb James?"

"We said hello a few times, during his representation. Broke my heart, the whole thing. The Lanes and the James have lived here forever, you know, and it like to tore the town apart. We all knew he had a drug problem, and it was so... scandalous. Men like Caleb, raised in a good home and went to a good school, they weren't supposed to have addictions, but there he was, skinny as can be. He'd lost *so* much weight."

"You knew him, didn't you. When he was younger," I said.

"Oh, well, Mr. August, it's a close community, and I've lived here my whole life. I met my husband on the playground at Heritage Elementary in the second grade. I'm younger than Caleb's parents, class of '84, and older than him, class of '09, but of course I knew them. And I cannot get over how big you are, Mr. August! You fill up the whole room, don't you."

"Steroids, Sally. Steroids."

She made a gasp. That would pass up and down the street like wildfire.

"Do you know Ervin Lane's family too?" I said.

"Well, of course I do."

"Of course you do," I said.

"Or at least I know *of* them. Not poor Kim Harper, never ran into her kin. They've only lived here one generation. She was sweet, though she thought us a little backward, but I believe the world could use a little backward, don't you."

"Preaching to the choir, Sally Gardner. I'm reading Wendell Berry, for heaven's sake," I said.

She still had my hand, and I wasn't sure if I'd ever get it back. But she was talking and I wouldn't do anything to stop the tea being spilled. "I won't pretend to know who that is, Mr. August."

"Kim Harper and Ervin Lane. Now that's an odd partnership, Sally."

"You're right, they do seem an odd fit, don't they," she said.

"You know what I wonder, Sally?"

"What's that, Mr. August?"

"Mackenzie."

A squeeze. Me and Sally, best buds.

"Mackenzie," she said.

"I wonder about Caleb and Ervin. I'm merely an obtuse outsider, you know. I wonder if they knew one another before that night."

"Do *not* answer that, Sally." Elaine Terry marched briskly through the front door without closing it. I recognized her from her website. She set her briefcase on top of Sally's desk and pointed at me. "Mackenzie August? I have five minutes. Come into my office, please."

It was my turn to squeeze, and I gave Sally a good one.

"Thanks for chatting," I said.

"Oh we weren't chatting, Mr. August. *Mackenzie*. I was seeing you out." She smiled and winked like she was a spy, a bad one in a comedy. "Don't be scared of her. She's not as mean as she lets on."

"I'm far worse than I seem. Now you have four minutes, Mr. August." She marched into her office, where she unleashed a loud sigh and she stretched toward the ceiling.

Elaine Terry had broad hips and narrow shoulders, so her suit fit at odd angles. Her hair was straight and blondish-white, and her teeth were new.

Inside her office, she talked at me. "You were hired to find Caleb James, right? But you're spending all your time on Court Street. I promise you, Mr. August, he is not here."

"Save me some time. Tell me where he is."

"I wouldn't possibly know the answer to that."

"Then he *could* be here. He could be upstairs," I said.

"I cannot help you. I don't know where Caleb went. And if I did, I would tell the U.S. Marshals, not you." She stood behind the desk and leaned on it.

"I'm looking for leads."

"How nice."

"Give me one," I said.

"No."

"Right now."

"No," she said.

"Did he and Ervin know one another as children?"

"The answer to that question will not help you locate Caleb James," she said.

"How do you know?"

"Please hunt elsewhere."

"The world is too wide. Gotta pick up his trail first," I said.

"Mr. August. I don't have time for this."

I grinned. I gave her the one reserved for press releases, if I ever had one. "We got off on the wrong foot, Ms. Terry."

"I have no time for any foot. And no, you may not call me Elaine."

"I was *about* to ask that."

"I could tell, and I foreclosed it. Mr. August—"

"Mackenzie."

"Mr. August, the murder of Kim Harper and maiming of Ervin Lane was a dark period for our town. I was hard gagged, and although the case is closed I still choose not to discuss it, even with friends," she said.

"Liar. You don't have friends."

Elaine didn't want to smile. But she did. A little.

"I have a few," she said.

"Those poor souls."

"They are long suffering. But I'm not. Get out. Go find a trail elsewhere."

"I'm heading to his parents' house."

"Ervin's parents are dead."

"I meant Caleb's parents," I said.

"Of course. Please don't harass him, Mr. August. Caleb's father has been through enough."

"Him? Is Caleb's father a widower? Maybe I won't if you divulge some information. Over a coffee?"

Behind us, a phone rang and Sally Gardner answered it quietly.

"You're cute, Mr. August," said Elaine Terry. "But I remain un-charmed. I'm not divulging a solitary fact."

"Do you know if he'd been skimming profits from his employer on Wall Street?"

"Get out."

"Caleb, I mean. Not Ervin."

"I *know* who you meant." Her phone rang. She grabbed it and said, "Elaine Terry. ...yes, Mr. Mendleson, good morning." She snapped twice with her fingers and pointed at the door.

"You want me to leave?" I said.

Two more snaps, more pointing. With vigor.

"What's the magic word?" I said.

She mouthed, GET OUT, which wasn't it, but I left anyway. I walked to the Great Food Mart on Grace Street and purchased for Sally Gardner a bouquet of yellow daises. I returned and set them on her desk and said, "For you. Not your boss. You are a delight."

Sally was still talking on the phone but she made a gasp, and I left, like Superman flying off into the blue.

## 7

I wanted coffee. The Mission Coffee House was only four blocks away, but it was near the bottom of the hill of Lynchburg and I was perched on the crest. If the town was a ski slope, it'd have been a black diamond, but I walked it anyway. At the bottom, feet hurting, I looked back up and decided I'd need to call an Uber to return.

The barista gave me a coffee and I sat at a table. I googled Caleb again on my phone, looking for information on his parents.

I found his mother in the obituaries. She died two years ago, mere months after Caleb was sent to Wallens Ridge. Renee James was survived by her beloved husband Walter and her son, Caleb. Jiminy Christmas.

Plus poor Walter had been a dentist.

No way Walter's business could survive his son's scandal. His clients would've bailed. He'd be a social outcast.

I googled Walter James and Dentistry, and sure enough he retired last year.

I was a father and my heart was pumping pure sympathy

for Walter. Son jailed, wife dead, business bankrupt, friends vanished...

I might bring Walter some flowers too. Or maybe a bottle of bourbon. Mackenzie August, the insensitive bastard, was gonna have to grill this grieving man in the coming days. I'd rather give nasty Elaine Terry a pedicure.

If I could find him. He'd most likely moved. I would've, if I was him.

I brought up Lynchburg deed transfers but there were too many to search the previous two years. Perhaps I could pester a realtor into assistance.

At the counter, I asked for a refill of coffee and I noticed a black and white photo of Caleb James on the cork board. It read, **Have you seen this man?** The feds were offering a five thousand dollar reward.

The barista caught me staring. "He used to come in here, you know."

"Caleb James did?"

"Before he had an office. He worked here some mornings," she said.

"You're the owner."

A nice-looking brunette woman about my age. She nodded.

"I'm looking for him," I said.

"To get the reward?"

"I'll split it with you."

She smiled and laughed through her nose.

I said, "I was hired to help. You have any clues, I'll take them."

"Wish I did have. Though he was always nice to us. Couldn't believe it when I heard," she said.

"Were you raised in Lynchburg?"

She nodded again.

"If you were Caleb, where would you hide?" I said.

"If I was Caleb, I'd find my ex-fiancée and beg her to take me back."

I did a gentleman's flinch and burned myself with the coffee and I set the mug down.

"Now you hold on one minute," I said.

She grinned, pleased with herself. She was washing portafilters from the cappuccino machine.

"Caleb was engaged?" I said.

"That juicy gossip always gets everyone," she said. "No one knew. I'm only telling you because you tipped a hundred percent for the coffee."

I shook my hand and sucked at the burn. "To whom was he engaged?"

"To whom?"

"Believe it or not, I read books in my free time."

"To whom." She was still smiling. "Robin Lucas."

"I'm surprised I didn't hear this in the news."

"No one knew. Most still don't. But she called it off."

"Why?" I said.

"Cause he was a druggie and a thief, why do you think?" said the barista. She set the metal filters into the drying rack, handles upward. "He and Robin dated in high school. He came back and they picked up where they left off. She was a teacher by then. She didn't detect the drug addiction at first, but when she did..." She made a throat slashing motion. "Pffft. She bailed. After Caleb was arrested, she left the state."

"Where'd she go?"

"You got me," she said. "I don't know anyone who knows."

"Did people blame her? Why'd she go into hiding?"

"Because of Ervin. The cop who got shot in the hand?"

"What about him?" I said.

"The rumor is, she left Caleb *for* Ervin."

I felt dizzy.

"Robin took up with Ervin?"

"That's what I heard. Wait." She stopped her cleaning. Frowned. "It was the other way around. Robin was with Ervin. But she left him. Took up with Caleb. Something like that, I can't remember. It was two and a half years ago, you know."

"Caleb's ex-fiancée had formerly dated Ervin. And Ervin shot him."

"Told you it was juicy. Anybody who knew, they blamed Robin. You can't be bestie-hopping and expect it to turn out well."

"Bestie-hopping?"

"Caleb and Ervin were childhood friends."

"*Childhood friends.*"

She took a second look at me. "Don't you know anything?"

"I..."

"I don't understand how you expect to find him if you didn't know that."

Mackenzie August. Speechless.

# 8

The Roanoke U.S. Marshal's office could pass for a police bull pen, but simpler. Whereas the police have an enormous range of responsibilities—enforce *all* laws (like traffic laws), prevent *all* crimes (like burglaries), respond to *all* emergencies (like murder and abuse)—the marshals have one primary role: deal with prisoners. Catch the guy and move him around. Ergo, their office was less complex with fewer moving parts and people.

Getting into the office was harder, though. Not only was there a sentry at the front desk, not only did he have to ring for Manny, but Manny had to satisfy two bio-security devices on the way back in, including a portal that locked on both ends and brought back unpleasant memories of prison.

Now he and I sat in rolling chairs at the desk of Sarah Underwood, a deputy U.S. Marshal who'd assisted Lynchburg in the Caleb James manhunt. Sarah looked like a marshal should—no patience for guff. Her shoulders and legs were strong from Ironman triathlons. Her hair was a high fade of bright blonde, and she had some scaring at the corner of her left eye; she took shrapnel in a gun battle last year, chasing a killer. I'd been there.

Sarah's boots were up on her desk and she leaned back in her chair, hands laced behind her head.

"He's got a better chance because he escaped alone. It's easier to bust out in a group, but groups are caught quicker. They argue, they split up, they turn on each other. Did you see *Reservoir Dogs*? These guys aren't sharp and they don't get along. Caleb James though..." Sarah shook her head. She looked through the wall and smiled fondly. "He's sharp."

"You're happy about it," I said.

"Better a crafty crook than a mundane one, know what I mean? I love a good chase."

"The Lynchburg guys." Manny make a tsk'ing noise with his teeth. "Not so sharp. Great Americans, but maybe too lazy."

"They're fine." Sarah shrugged. "They didn't know what to do with me, an outsider, but I liked them. Not everyone gets caught. Statistically we catch less then seventy-percent of runaways."

"Even with great hair? You two could be on a barber's poster," I said.

"Hard to believe, isn't it," said Sarah.

"I'm still early in this, but Caleb made a few mistakes," I said. "He got lucky it didn't cost him."

"Going back to Lynchburg, yeah. Dumb move, but we think he was protecting his father. Caleb made a killing before the lockup, so to speak. A windfall off crypto. Waiting for trial, he arranged to transfer the money to his parents. Fast-forward two years, his father withdrew a bunch of cash and stored it in a safe-deposit box at the post office. After Caleb busted loose, he took the money from the box. It's hard to catch a fugitive and it's near impossible if he's got money."

"How much?" I asked.

"His father said a hundred grand. Bank receipts match it."

"A Lynchburg safe-deposit box?"

"Yep."

"If his father had made the deposit in Big Stone Gap, he'd look guilty. By doing it in Lynchburg, he could claim Caleb robbed him," I said.

She pointed at me. I liked it.

"Bingo," she said. "Caleb supposedly broke into his old man's house, found the key, and took the cash without his father's permission. The old man says he likes access to cash, and the safe-deposit box was safer than under his mattress. It's bullshit, but it's feasible, so we can't charge him with anything. Not that we would."

Manny nodded his approval.

"Good fathers help sons, even fugitives. I like this guy," he said.

"We watched the video of Caleb at the post office, and we tried to follow him on traffic cameras but no dice. He was on a bicycle," she said.

"How'd he look?"

"Healthier than his trial. Fewer drugs in prison."

"Since then, no credit cards, no passports, no driver's license, nothing," I said.

"Nothing."

"Did he burn down Ervin's house before or after the post office?"

"Ervin's house burned down on a Wednesday evening. He accessed the post office box on Thursday," said Sarah.

"When did he visit the drug dealer?"

"Thursday or Friday, I can't remember. After the fire. Then, *poof*. He's gone."

"Why didn't you help?" I asked Manny.

"Ay, he'd be caught by now."

Sarah laughed.

"Manny was on one of his don't-ask, don't-tell trips. Him and Beck. We hope they're banging, but they swear they aren't."

I scanned the wide office, including Noelle Beck's desk. Their desks were pushed together so they faced each other. Hers had two big computer screens. His had an unopened box of leather Peter Millar loafers. "Where is she?"

Manny rolled his eyes and he shifted his shoulders, irritated. "She took a personal day, like they do in France. *Endeble*."

"Rocky Rickard is in town." Sarah grinned at Manny. "Good-looking guy, rich, older, crazy about Beck. Even I'd take his call."

"I like the *hombre*. He's a capitalist and he's got style. But he's a major league criminal, and Beck gets knocked-up out of wedlock, like they do in France, I gotta raise the baby, cause Rocky will run. Criminal *pendejos* take no responsibility. Like they do in France."

"What's with France?" said Sarah.

"They beat Puerto Rico in a friendly," I said.

"Soccer?"

"*Si. Futball*," I said.

"A coincidence, only. France sucks all the time," said Manny.

I steered us back on topic.

"You think Caleb's in Mexico?"

"Probably. Caleb mentioned it to the dealer Marky. And

even though his father said they haven't spoken, his father mentioned Mexico too. If he's smart, he is. And he's smart."

"How long before the breakout did his father stuff the deposit box?" I said.

"Twenty days."

"Prison phone records?"

"Caleb called his father once every month. They're recorded, and I listened to the six prior to Caleb's breakout. He and his old man said a few odd things, like talking in code, but nothing blatant or incriminating. I can get you the files," she said.

"How'd he set fire to Ervin's house?"

"A trashcan in the garage. Lit the contents and pushed it next to the wall."

"Why did he set fire to the house of a cop he shot? This part makes no sense to me," I said.

"Makes no damn sense to anyone, not unless Caleb was already out of his mind on meth. Which is possible," she said.

"They were childhood friends. Caleb and Ervin. Did you know that?"

"I didn't." She rolled her eyes. Her hands were still behind her head. "Lynchburg Marshals didn't see fit to tell me, I guess, though I don't know it would've changed anything on my end."

"They had history. I think they hated each other."

"I don't know. I'm not in the detecting business. I catch the bastards, that's it."

Manny was less talkative than usual, but now he said, "He wanted to kill Ervin, why'd he start a fire? Why not shoot him?"

"Ervin's bigger. A cop. Trained with a gun," I said.

"Caleb's none of those things. Didn't want to risk it, is my guess. If he even set the fire. No one saw him do it."

"Be a big coincidence."

"A big damn coincidence," said Sarah.

"You talked to Ervin?" I said.

"I did."

"When?"

Sarah searched the ceiling for the answer. "A few times. I flew out there a month after he moved. Me and a Lynchburg guy. Ervin's not in WITSEC, but we all feel some responsibility, you know what I mean. He's a cop."

"How was he?"

"Drunk. He's always drunk now. Drunk and angry. He told me to get lost and not to come back, so I didn't." She released some airy frustration upward, a blast of air. "They were childhood friends. Jesus. That's why we haven't caught Caleb. Lynchburg circled their wagons. It's an in-house problem, so they want to deal with it in-house. This whole shit-show, it's a good example of a small town trying to protect itself. Lynchburg isn't that small, but the law enforcement community is. You know? They didn't want outsiders like CNN or Fox getting hold of their dirty laundry."

"Did you know Caleb had been engaged?"

She took the boots off her desk and sat up straight, hard enough the chair rolled backwards.

"You're shitting me."

"Only lasted a few months," I said. "She called it off."

"Those..." She stood up. "Those got'damn country boys, not telling me... Damn it, got'damn it."

"Ten bucks says, if you ask them, they'll claim they followed her up."

"Of course they'll say that."

"And they most likely did," I said.

"Still."

"Still. It's another secret."

"That office is nothing but men. Men from the country. Nice guys, but... To be honest, they didn't know the hell to do with a lesbian with better hair." She made a fist and punched her desk lightly twice.

Manny withdrew the cell phone from his pocket and snapped a photo of his colleague. "Angry Sarah is my favorite Sarah."

"You're a freak, Martinez."

I said, "That street, Court Street, it has secrets."

"Hell yeah they do."

"The judge gagged everyone, the prosecutor doesn't want me to see the video, the defense attorney refused to answer questions, the marshal's office didn't tell you Caleb'd been engaged..."

"What could they be hiding? They arrest a guy driving under the influence and he attacks them," said Sarah. "Where's the big secret?"

"My working theory is Ervin botched the arrest. Maybe their childhood friendship led to a lapse in judgment. Maybe..."

"Maybe the arresting office, Ervin, he was drunk," said Manny.

We fell silent.

For a couple reasons.

Out of respect for the fallen—a woman had been killed in the line of duty.

Out of respect for the hellacious job it was to arrest someone on meth.

And out of respect for something Sarah said earlier—we all felt some responsibility. If Ervin had erred, and it got his partner killed... it was hard to blame the police for covering it up. You frisk enough cops, you'll find some carrying flasks. It's a hard job, and they have each other's back.

After the moment of silence, I carried on.

"Even if Ervin botched the arrest, Caleb killed an officer and he's on the run. Catching him would be the jewel in the crown of my career."

"What if he's in Mexico?" said Sarah.

"Then he's in luck."

"You won't follow?" she said.

"No. It's summer, and Mexico is too hot."

"*Ay caramba*, you're a wimp."

"How can I help?" said Sarah.

"I need to talk to Caleb's father."

She opened her laptop and clicked a few things. She removed a notecard from her top drawer and scribbled on it.

"Here," she said, "is his address. And I'm writing down Ervin Lane's too, out in Indiana. Those Lynchburg assholes might not share, but I will."

"Thanks." I did *not* want to pester Caleb's poor father. But I would.

"Good luck with this," she said.

"Real men make their own luck," said Manny. "*Sí?*"

"I wouldn't know. I can't even make duck l'orange. But I'll take your word for it."

## 9

Ronnie and I tied our Nike laces on the front porch, Kix waiting patiently in his jogging stroller. Two years ago, it'd swallowed him whole. Last year, it'd been roomy. Now he looked like a fat guy in a phone booth.

Ronnie fetched GPA from the house and I took the stroller and we started west on Windsor, jogging at a nine-minute-mile pace deeper into the neighborhood. It was after seven and the day's humidity had lifted, and Grandin had great sidewalks. We stayed on our street until it ended at Edgewood and turned right and came back east on Maiden Lane, then back on Westover, zigzagging slowly northward in serpentine fashion.

Ronnie was a natural athlete, light on her feet and trim and quick. The same way Manny was, both of them built like a sleek Porsche, whereas I was more of a diesel truck. Her footfalls barely made a sound, as though she wore better shoes than me. Which she *didn't*. She could've accelerated but she didn't, and I felt no shame about it, and we finished three miles later at the elementary school, and she walked in a circle, checking her pulse and smiling. I sat down hard on a bench, drenched, and I didn't care if I had a pulse.

Kix took off for a staircase that led to a plastic slide and GPA followed anxiously.

"Mackenzie, do you remember that card game," said Ronnie, her chest rising and falling smoothly, like she wasn't about to die, "when a man named Dexter tried to murder me, but you intervened?"

I nodded. "I do."

"You tore his throat open. You held his muscles and his arteries in your fingers. It was awful."

"He tried to hurt my girl."

"I wasn't your girl then," she said.

"It was a foregone conclusion. In fact, you'd announced to the room you loved me."

"You remember."

"Had you asked, I could've flown," I said.

"I'd known it a while, but that was my first public disclosure."

Ronnie had a patina in her cheeks from the jog. Some days she took a long lunch and lounged at the Roanoke Country Club pool for an hour. She wasn't a member but they granted her access anyway, and she was tan from it. A cute ribbon of light freckles lay over her nose.

"Sometimes, when you're cooking soup or putting Kix to bed, I forget you're that guy. The guy who can pull Dexter's neck apart with his thumbs."

"I didn't enjoy it," I said.

"But you did it. You are capable of extreme violence. Of things you don't want to do."

Kix called for us to watch and he zoomed down the slide. At the bottom, GPA licked his face and Kix shouted at her. He stood and waddled to the slide again.

"Why are you dwelling on that?" I said.

"I don't know."

"But."

"I'm having a minor crisis," said Ronnie. "It's minor, but it's real."

"Your friend Charlotte Andrew's divorce."

"You're quite perceptive, Mackenzie."

"Perspicacious is the sexier word there."

She bent at the waist to stretch, my callipygian wife, and I admired it until she finished and sat beside me.

I said, "You don't want to do divorce work anymore?"

"That's not it."

"There will always be divorces, and always a need for good people to be their lawyers."

"Clever." She smiled to herself, looking at her ankles. "You said good people, not good lawyers."

"In the case of a divorce with children involved, both sides would be wise to hire the former, and the rest will figure itself out, seems to me."

"I don't mind divorce work. But not Charlotte's."

"Because she's obtuse?" I said.

Kix fell at the top of the slide and landed on his butt and zipped down before he was ready. He reached the bottom, GPA lapped him in the face again, and Kix shouted. The fall and sudden slide startled him, and he wondered if he shouldn't have some consolation from his father. I told him he was okay, and he believed me. No babying required. GPA licked him again and Kix hit her in the head, and he told her to knock that crap off, and he started for the stairwell again, GPA trailing closely, undeterred.

"It's not only that she's obtuse. It's that..." Ronnie raised her hands in front of her, like trying to feel something unseen. "I like her. Or I used to, when we were young, and maybe I still do. And I wish for her something better than what she has. Or is."

"You don't mean a better husband."

"I think I wish for her a better version of herself. And if I help her divorce, I'm enabling the poorer version." She lowered the hands to her knees. "I want her to grow. To move closer to the ideal."

"And divorce won't help that."

"I don't know her husband. I'm not judging her or him, and I'm not moralizing. There's a truth here that I'm flirting with, but can't pinpoint. Do you know what it is?"

"Not yet," I said. "Is it related to killing Dexter?"

"It must be, Mackenzie, though I don't know how."

"It'll come to you. Let the mind work in the background," I said.

"Is your mind working? About catching what's-his-name?"

"Caleb. And yes."

"Tell me?"

"I don't know much, other than I suspect I uprooted a mystery within the mystery," I said.

"Ooooh, go on."

"It's difficult to disappear. We humans need connection, and we have habits, and we make mistakes. I'm looking for Caleb's connections and habits and mistakes, and in the process I discovered that Lynchburg is probably hiding something."

"Tomorrow is only day three of the investigation? And you're already finding secrets."

"I found the dim evidence of a secret, at best. But I don't know whose it is, nor the nature of it. Did the arresting officer make a mistake? Did the prosecutor err? Why else would the cop-killer receive such a light sentence? I am adrift in questions and no answers."

Kix returned to our bench, shepherded by the dog. Kix had mulch tangled in his hair and stuffed down his shirt.

*I fell again. And you missed it. Somehow that makes it worse.*

"This guy's a mess," said Ronnie. "Ready to return home?"

*Please. I am mortified.*

I forced myself up and I groaned doing it.

"Let's call for a car."

"No way, buster," she said. "I like it when you're sweaty."

*Dear lord, I am a child and do not want to hear this.*

"I'll race you home, and our minds will be working in the background, like you said," said Ronnie.

"We could stroll sedately and do the same thing."

"The Mackenzie I love isn't afraid of hard work."

"If we're racing, you push the stroller this time," I said.

"Deal."

I leaned down and unclipped the front wheel of the stroller. The wheel rolled free and fell sideways, and ol' Mackenzie August had himself an advantage. Kix accused me of cheating and Ronnie accused me of being something worse. I jogged out of the park while Ronnie threw mulch at me and picked up the wheel to reattach it to the stroller.

Though a prince among men, I still lost by four blocks.

## 10

I caught a flight the next morning at 7:15 out of Roanoke on a small Delta jet, half full. The stewardesses wore masks and emanated all the warmth they could from their eyes. The flight lasted an hour and a half, providing enough time to eat a bag of crackers and drink one delicious ginger ale in a plastic cup. We landed at Hartsfield-Jackson Atlanta, one of the bigger airports in the world. The guy across from me said the square footage of the airport was bigger than the square footage of downtown Atlanta, which would've blown my hat off had I been wearing one.

An hour layover in Atlanta, and I lifted off for Evansville, Indiana, and another round of crackers and soda, and I napped for twenty minutes. We landed at a charming regional airport and I rented a Chevy Cruze and drove it north into Daviess County.

Daviess was a rolling land and devoted solely to agriculture. I traveled on Interstate 69 for five minutes at a time without passing a car, and when I did it was a truck. Farmland as far as I could see, with great machines crawling across them, spewing water on soybeans or harvesting corn. I knew from research last night that much of the population was Amish and I was eager to see them and explain I was reading Wendell Berry and be accepted among them.

After an hour, I arrived in Washington, Indiana, one of those sleepy communities the world didn't know existed, and both sides were happy with the arrangement. The town had little new construction, but the old buildings were maintained with pride and new white paint and surrounded by bright green lawns. Classic Americana. Women stood outside the Stitching Post with new fabric, and men sat on chairs at The White Steamer with hamburgers and soda in glass bottles, and kids on bicycles raced towards North Elementary on 5th Street, under an unbroken dome of infinite peacock.

Everyone waved or watched me pass. Wondering, I assume, if I was Tom Hardy here to film a movie about farming.

I turned west on Cosby, drove for a mile further into the past, into the deep wild Midwest of corn, then south on Akester, and reached my destination after six hours of travel.

The new home of Ervin Lane.

I parked in the gravel alongside the road with the windows down, and breathed in the heady aroma of cow. No traffic in sight, and no sounds other than the click of my engine. The road vanished into points in the distance in both directions, dividing a sea of jade.

Ervin Lane owned several acres of earth and lived in a double-wide trailer, as did the two neighbors I could see. A newish Ford F-150 was parked beside the trailer. A one-story barn out back, painted red, plus a shed, fencing, and a pigpen, all of it in tiptop shape. His plot of land looked organized and cared for, as though benefiting from an industrious homesteader.

I'd been expecting to find the slum of a drunk, and I was wrong about it.

Ervin himself stood in the back yard, visible from my spot alongside the road. He was feeding chickens until he saw me. He raised to stretch his back and he waved at me with his right hand. His left arm held the bucket of feed.

I stood out of the car and I stretched too. The tall sky and flat world made me feel tiny.

Ervin watched me uncertainly as I walked up his gravel drive and around the truck.

"Afternoon," he said. "Do I know you?"

"You don't. But I came a long way, and I think we're friends." I raised my hands at his little farm. "This is worth the trip. Makes me rethink Suburbia."

He transferred the bucket to his right hand, and he set it down.

"My slice of Eden," he said.

"Cultivating the land and working hard, as God intended."

"That's it. That's exactly it. Thirsty? I have iced tea. Or lemonade. And milk was delivered this morning."

"Ervin," I said, "nothing sounds better in this pastoral paradise than a glass of lemonade."

He grinned. "Meet me at the house."

I walked across his grass while he took a longer route around the fencing, scattering a dozen chickens. Beyond them were pigs in a pen, not looking at me.

Ervin walked through a vegetable garden, closing gates as he came, and stepped out of his muddy boots and into an old pair of Reeboks.

His left hand was a hard plastic prosthesis. Big and probably reinforced to hold things like the back end of a rake or the handle of a bucket. His head was shaved and his goatee was trim. A few tattoos peeked at the sunlight from his collar and sleeves.

"Your accent. Where's it from?" he said. "If you don't mind."

"I spent some time in Louisiana as a kid. The rest of it in Roanoke, Virginia."

He stopped at the rear door to his trailer. His modern and well-appointed trailer, by the look of it.

"Roanoke."

"Yeah," I said.

"I can guess what brings you, can't I."

"Probably. And I'm sorry for it."

"Caleb," he said.

"I'm a private cop, pitching in, trying to find him."

We stood for several heartbeats too many, regarding the other. He was stiff and tense.

Then, "Lemonade, you said?"

I nodded.

"If you're still offering."

"Sure." He pointed at one of the Adirondack chairs facing away from the trailer, kinda northwest with a good view of sunsets. "Take a load off."

He stepped inside and the screen door slapped closed behind. Beside the door was a little window, probably set over the kitchen sink, and taped to the interior side of the window was a pink heart, handmade. A local girlfriend?

His appearance shocked me. Instead of a bloated drunk, Ervin was a hale, active specimen of a man. In the photos he was heavy and swollen—not now. He'd lost thirty pounds and gained the benefits from it.

Inside I heard him murmuring into a phone and he

returned three minutes later with two glass jars of lemonade, both held in his right hand. I took mine and offered my
credentials.

He read the license. "Mackenzie August. Private
detective."

"That's me."

"Who hired you?"

"Wealthy Baptist socialites."

He returned the wallet and he kinda laughed. "Did
they."

"They want the man who shot your hand off returned to
prison."

Ervin lowered into his chair. "Sounds like Samantha
Miller."

"You know her," I said.

"I do. It's amazing, you give a pretty girl some money and
she thinks the whole damn world is her business. Her
interest isn't me or justice. It's because Caleb went to a
church on the side opposite hers."

"I don't think her aims are dishonest, but probably more
aggrandizing than she'd care to admit."

"Any luck so far? With Caleb?" he said.

"Not much. That's why I'm here."

"I asked them not to send anyone. I asked to be left
alone."

"I know, Ervin, and I feel gross about it. I'm normally a
pain in the ass, but this one time I'll leave the second you
say the word. You've been through hell. Though to be
honest, you look great."

He rapped the knuckles of his good hand on the hard
prosthetic one.

"Most of me," he said.

"Other than the missing parts, you look great."

He laughed and drank some lemonade.

"Clean living. Amazing what farm life will do."

"It suits you. Does it pay the bills?" I said.

"No but I get a check from my medical retirement once a month, and at night I clean Lena Dunn Elementary. I'm a custodian and, believe it or not, I love the job. It all works out to more than enough."

"More than enough," I said, "is a good way to describe Eden."

"You traveled a long way, Detective, and I don't mean to rush you, but how do I help?"

"Caleb's done a solid job of disappearing. I'm looking into his life and the night of the arrest, hoping to connect some dots. Two things don't make sense to me. Maybe you can help with one or both."

He nodded and stretched his back again, like he was sore.

"The first thing," I said, "is that Lynchburg is hiding something about that night. And I want to know what it is."

"You mean, when Kim and I arrested him."

"The prosecutor doesn't want me to watch the dashcam. Caleb's defense attorney told me to get out. The police chief refused to give me your address. The marshals aren't sharing information," I said.

"They closed ranks."

"What's the reason for it?"

Ervin didn't respond. His eyes were on the northwestern horizon. He drank lemonade without thinking about it and wiped his mouth with his left forearm. The prosthetic hand was attached with a hard plastic socket sleeve, ending halfway to his elbow.

"Did you try one of those robotic hands that moves?" I said.

He nodded without taking his eyes off the distance.

"Didn't like it. Maybe I'll try again one day, if it's not too late. But I'm fine the way I am," he said. "What's the other thing? That I might help with."

"Caleb broke out of prison and came after you. Set fire to your house. Why the hell'd he do that?"

Ervin sniffed. "Good question."

"You two have history. You were childhood friends."

"That ended a long time ago. We drifted apart. Different guys going different directions. It had nothing to do with that evening," he said.

"Seems like he hated you, though, Ervin."

"Asking about my childhood friendships won't help you catch a fugitive."

"The world's too big to go knocking door to door. Gotta start somewhere. Gotta find some angle the marshal's aren't taking. I don't have facial recognition software, so I chase relationships."

"You think Caleb will try again," he said.

"He might."

Ervin drained his glass and the ice tinkled against the side. He stood and walked indoors. I heard the fridge open, and a minute later he came out with a refill. Mine was still half full and I sipped some. It was cloyingly sweet.

He set his jar down.

"What do you know about heroin and the Vietnam War?"

"Nothing," I said.

"Vietnam was hell on the men who went, obviously. The GIs took drugs to get through the day. And through the jungle. Heroin was the narcotic of choice over there. Whole battalions came home addicted to it, and heroin is a dependency you don't quit. The Army was scrambling to figure out how to deal with all these heroin-heads returning to small towns. But you know what happened?" He snapped the fingers of his right hand. "They stopped. Like that. Ninety-five percent did. Isn't that wild? Only five percent stayed addicted, and these were the guys already doing drugs before the war. Turns out, a man doesn't need will power. What he needs is to be removed from temptation. Take him out of his Army tent, full of smack, and send him home, where there is none, and he'll quit."

"I need to move to a land where cookies are outlawed," I said.

He carried on, like I wasn't hilarious.

"I pulled Caleb over that night," he said, "and I was drunk. Drunk off my ass. I was drunk every day before that, and most days since. Up until five months ago. Now I'm sober."

"You go to a local AA group?"

"Once a week, in Washington, ten minutes away. Moving out here..." He indicated the farm and the world around it with his prosthesis. Poised like he wanted to continue, like he had more to say. Something about the enormity of life and the seconds ticking by and their inexpressible importance. But the moment passed and he lowered against the back of his chair, looking at his farm like seeing it fresh, and we sat in silence several minutes.

I drank more lemonade.

"I'm glad he escaped," said Ervin quietly.

Mackenzie August, caught flatfooted. Of all the things I thought he might utter...

"I'm glad Caleb escaped and I hope you don't find him. I was drunk that night, and everything would be different if I hadn't been."

"Maybe that's why Caleb wants revenge," I said.

"Can you blame him?"

"I don't know. I don't know the whole story."

"I've forgiven him and I hope he's forgiven me, or that he's working on it." Ervin was smiling now. "I hope he's far away. I hope he's on a beach or his own plot of land, and he's content and safe. Safe from you and the marshals."

"He's a cop killer."

Ervin flinched.

"He was a meth junkie and he blew off your hand and he killed Kim Harper," I said. It sounded lame to my ears but it was a truth we were ignoring.

"I didn't say he was innocent. But I'm a lot more interested in my life than his." Ervin stood. "I don't mean to be rude, Detective, but I'm done talking. I won't answer any more questions."

I'd come here for answers, and he'd given me a glimpse, but that was all. His newfound peace, while heathy for him, made my job trickier. I had a hundred acute follow-up redirections and no way to press them, because I'd said I would leave when asked.

I made a nodding notion.

He was half facing away from me, revealing the tattoo on the back of his neck. Looked like a blue police badge—maybe Kim Harper's?

His right hand on the door. "I appreciate it if you don't go asking questions around town. They're skeptical enough about me, the outsider who arrived drunk."

"You bet." I pulled a card from my wallet and pinned the corner under my lemonade jar. "My number's on there, if you change your mind."

"I won't. Safe flight home, Detective."

As he went inside, I caught a glimpse of a pistol tucked

under his shirt at the small of his back. Maybe his former service piece?

Had he gone inside earlier to get it? Was he dealing with PTSD?

Of course he was. Dumb-ass question.

I walked to my rental, alone with a long journey ahead. From the passenger window, I had enough of an angle to see him emerge again. Collect my lemonade jar. And tear my business card in half.

## 11

The fact that Ervin was drunk that night answered a lot of questions.

No wonder the prosecutor Terrance Goodwin hadn't wanted me to see the dashcam video—the arresting officer was inebriated. I had to assume Elaine Terry—Caleb's defense attorney—had seen it. That's why Caleb had been convicted of second degree murder, instead of capital. A plea deal. If Elaine had been a bit more tenacious, it was probable she could've gotten the whole thing dismissed. I wondered if she'd tried.

It also explained why Ervin had moved to Indiana and nearly drank himself to death before joining AA—he was partially responsible for Kim Harper's death.

His drunkenness didn't excuse Caleb from pulling a gun and killing Kim Harper though. Nor did it help me find Caleb.

But it did give me a bargaining chip with Caleb's father, Skip James, the widower, social outcast, and retired dentist.

I pulled into his driveway the next morning, having located him with the address provided by Sarah Underwood and her slighted pride. Skip lived in the mountains north of Lynchburg, in Amherst, in a secluded group of log cabins that you couldn't see from the road. The neighbors were hidden from one another unless you walked a quarter mile through the poplar and pine. These weren't rustic cabins—the luxury kits were purchased from a magazine and brought partially assembled.

Two thousand feet above sea level, built on the southern slopes, shaded and cool in the morning, thirty minutes from town, a good place for a grieving widower to hide. And I the snooping detective come to ruin it. I stood beside my Accord and listened to the forest of birdcalls, and my clicking engine, alien and intrusive. From the drive, I could see a corner of his backyard, a little flat grassy spot.

"I recognize you, sir. And you aren't welcome."

Skip James was drinking coffee on his front porch, sitting in a rocking chair. He was thin, like his son, and had all his hair, dark flecked with gray.

"I'm here for a root canal, Dr. James."

He did not smile. Which was outrageous.

"I took a call two days ago, telling me you were poking around, the inspector in those articles. And now you're here, at my unlisted home, which portends nothing good. I'd appreciate it if you got back into your car."

"If you demand it, I will. But as revenge, I'll gargle with Pepsi," I said.

"You may think this is funny. You may think you're funny, but I don't."

I held up my hands and ducked my head, like—*okay, okay.*

"I have a son," I said. "Some of the stuff you've dealt with as a father, I can imagine. And some I can't. If a man like me came looking for my son, I'd be tempted to beat him to death."

"So you understand the situation." He eased in the rocking chair onto his left hip, enough so he could pull a holstered pistol off his belt and set it on the wooden railing.

"I have one too. It's in the car. I'd like to handle this conversation civilly."

"I don't give one got'damn what you like," he said. "You try to go round back, you try to snoop, I'll kill you. Leave."

"I will."

"Good."

"As soon as I tell you my bargaining chip," I said.

"I don't give one got'damn about that either."

"Ervin was drunk the night he pulled Caleb over."

Skip made a snort through his nose.

"I know that. A lot of people know, but in that town? The cops are too tight a fraternity."

"What if I could prove it?"

Skip's eyebrows raised. He slowly rocked back in his chair and drank from his mug. "What if you could?"

"The arresting officer was drunk, Dr. James. The thirty-year sentence Caleb received is a lot, considering. I know a better lawyer than Elaine Terry."

"I don't follow. Why exactly are you trespassing on my property, Inspector?"

"I have an idea. We cut a deal."

"What deal?"

"I find dispositive evidence that Ervin was drunk that night. We get an outside lawyer—one not under the influence of Court Street—to negotiate with the state. We won't go public with the evidence of drunkenness if Caleb gets a reduced sentence."

Skip set the mug on the slats of the porch and he stood.

Leaned forward on the railing, looking straight down into the mulch bed. Thinking.

"A reduced sentence," he said.

"They'll find him, Dr. James. The marshals are good at this. Better we cut him a deal before they do."

"Sounds to me like you want Caleb to turn himself in."

"In exchange for a reduced sentence," I said. "And the promise we don't blow the whistle on Ervin."

"How could you prove Ervin Lane was drunk? The police chief, he already knows. So does the prosecution. Hell, so does Elaine Terry, but a fat lot of good it did my son."

"He got thirty-years instead of life or the electric chair, so that's something. But not enough." I was still standing on the drive below him, looking up, like a supplicant.

"How could you prove it?"

"I'm good at my job. Super good."

"You'd be angering an entire town of cops. Sounds like a dangerous thing," he said.

"It would be."

"But you'd do it anyway? Why?"

"I keep my word. I was hired to catch Caleb."

It was the wrong thing to say. I heard the words at the same time he did and we both hated them.

"But that's only part of it," I said. "This whole thing is a disaster. Caleb was high. Ervin was drunk. Kim's dead. The prosecution and the judge suppressed evidence. A shit show. No one wants the whole thing dug up. But there's a quiet way forward for Caleb where he doesn't get out of jail when he's sixty."

His skin had tensed around the eyes and mouth, and he wasn't relaxing.

"A reduced sentence," he said.

"Something less than thirty."

"How about zero? How about he never goes to prison again."

"He shot a cop, Dr. James," I said.

"You can die and burn in hell, Inspector. He did no such thing."

"He pled guilty to it."

"He doesn't remember anything from that night. Did you know that? Fuck you and your reduced sentence." Skip's face was stark white. "They forced my son to confess to something he didn't do."

I didn't want to press on. I didn't want to aggravate this open wound. I didn't want to hurt this father more than he already had been. But sometimes life is awful and we do hard things.

"If Caleb was high," I said, "and he doesn't remember anything, then how do you know he's innocent of the thing he confessed to?"

"BECAUSE I KNOW MY SON!"

I stepped backwards involuntarily.

The forest soaked up the scream, but somewhere above us his words echoed. The mountain was full of hurt.

"Fathers know their children!" He pounded on the railing with a fist. The pistol fell off and thudded in the mulch. "Drug addiction doesn't make a man a killer! It doesn't make a man violent, either, not necessarily!"

What about the rumor that Caleb stole from his financial firm in New York City? Or that Caleb attacked a deputy in prison? That his fiancée left him? That Caleb tried to kill Ervin by burning down his house?

These were questions a competent detective with a heart of black coal would ask.

Instead I took another step backward, toward my car.

"They'll find him, Dr. James," I said.

"Like hell they will. My boy is too smart. He's in Mexico."

"Tell him my offer."

"I can't," he said. "My phone is being monitored by the marshals, we both know that."

"Tell him I can prove Ervin was drunk, somehow, and that'll get him a better deal, but he has to be willing to surrender. See what he says. My phone number is easy to find."

"I *won't*. I can't..."

Skip lowered his head to the railing and sobbed.

Mackenzie August practically jumped into his car and closed the door.

Good grief. I'd rather be in a car wreck than do that again.

I slid the key into the ignition, staring through the windshield and taking deep breaths. At that moment, if Caleb had been in the car with me, I wasn't sure if I would've turned him in. For the sake of his father. His father who lost his wife and son and who'd retreated from the world to a cabin on a mountain with a...

With a flat grassy spot behind the cabin.

I DROVE a quarter mile to Skip's neighbor. Three cars were parked in the drive and a woman stood out front and she watered her flower garden. I rolled by them to the next house. This one was vacant, a For Sale sign staked at the road. I parked there.

A little flat grassy spot.

*You go round back, you try to snoop, I'll kill you.*

I popped the trunk and traded my Nikes for hiking boots

and I laced them tight. I walked back toward Skip's, half a mile, and when I drew near I turned into the woods. The earth was damp with a wetness that remained for days after a rain, covered by the canopy above. Poplar and pine. It meant I could move quietly, and I walked Skip's property line, keeping in sight of the house, barely, my boots and jeans getting muddy. The hike from the road to his house was at a steep incline, another quarter mile because of the long drive, and I was sucking air, my feet sore, when I reached a spot level with his backyard.

Hands on my knees, I filled my lungs, in and out, for two minutes until my pulse recovered. Did Sam Spade ever pass out from walking up a mountain? I couldn't remember. Spenser might have, never Hawk, though. Too bad I was Spenser in this situation.

I crept closer through the wet undergrowth, tearing denim on thorns, until I had a good view. The flat grassy spot was small, framed by a stone retaining wall that kept the mountain from tumbling in. The space would take ten minutes to mow, some of it occupied by a concrete patio.

Back here, Skip kept a charcoal grill. A hose, coiled at the spigot. A rocking chair. A small plastic shed where the mower was kept. And a child's playhouse and slide, the colorful brand. Little Tikes. Perfect for a toddler.

*You go round back, I'll kill you.*

Skip James, widower, one son on the lam, had a play-set he didn't want me to see.

*Hey-o!* A clue.

I loved those.

## 12

The drive from Amherst took two hours, and I spent the duration feeling worse about myself. True, I'd found a clue, but I wrecked a man's week to get it. I parked at my office and pretended to work until lunch. I had emails to send, calls to make, papers to serve, but I didn't want to do them. I wanted to stare at the ceiling with loathing and disgust of my profession.

Which I did.

Like all things I did, I did it well.

For twenty minutes I indulged in self-pity and thoughts of moving to St. Pete Beach and working at a private airport with my dog and sleeping in a hammock and buying a seaplane and getting a pilot's license and flying tourists around the Gulf of Mexico and drinking everything out of a coconut with a straw.

Then I recalled that Ronnie says paradise is best visited, instead of exhausted, and I checked the humidity in Florida and good grief.

Instead of chasing the coconut dream, I got a pineapple smoothie from Elderberry's and I motored home.

Ronnie's red Mercedes C-Class was in the driveway and the girl herself paused on the steps.

"My husband," she said.

I closed my car door. Like all things, I did it well. "My Ronnie."

"You're home."

"As are you. What great detectives we are."

"My two afternoons canceled." She gave me and the Honda an inspection. "No Kix?"

"It's his nap time. I'll pick him up after."

Her eyes hovered on my face and I felt her attention like a warm zephyr.

"You're upset," she said.

"I do not get upset."

"I am a student of yours, Mackenzie. I study you like a schoolgirl does her favorite subject. I know when you're upset."

"A lesser man would be."

She set down the satchel she'd been carrying. "You're sad. I feel it all the way to my womb when you're sad."

"To do my job, I made a man cry. A father. A widower. I am a storm of self-recrimination."

"Remind me. Ervin Lane's father?"

I stopped on the first step, looking up at her on the porch. "Caleb James's father."

She placed her hands on my cheeks. "It was difficult. And painful."

"It was."

"You need healing," she said.

"A lesser man would need it."

"Mackenzie," she said. "I want to help you heal."

"Do you."

She still held my face. "I do. Can you guess what I'm insinuating?"

"I have an idea."

"Let's do it together, me and you. For two," she said, "whole hours."

"Ronnie."

She kissed my mouth. "Just say yes. You know I love to, in the afternoons."

"Ronnie."

"It's been a long time, Mackenzie. Please."

"It's a tremendous idea. But I'm not sure if I can, for two hours."

"The man I married could," she said.

"Let's say, ninety minutes."

"Your ninety-minute suggestion has been ratified." She grabbed my hand and tugged me inside. Following Ronnie up the stairs was one of my favorite pastimes. We took turns in the bathroom, and when I arrived to my bedroom she was already under the covers, disrobed, and beaming from her pillow. She said, "Ninety minutes."

"I'm so excited it's unmanly."

"Making your darling wife happy is never unmanly." She flipped the covers down. "Lose the clothes please. All of them, and get in bed."

I undressed and she made the correct noises of appreciation, though we both knew I hadn't been to the gym in a few weeks. I slid next to her, forming a pair of spoons, and put my arm around her and pulled her in and squeezed until she squeaked.

She spoke into her pillow. "This is the happiest I've ever been."

"Shhh," I said.

"Yes Mackenzie."

Giddy like we'd done something wrong, warm, our bodies touching everywhere, the blankets a shield from the world, she fell asleep first, and I smiled to myself, and soon followed her.

FOR DINNER THAT NIGHT, I chopped ten hearts of romaine lettuce and built a small mountain of green. Next to the lettuce were bowls of accoutrements—cubes of grilled chicken and flank steak, mozzarella cheese crisps, shredded cheddar, garlic croutons, veggies, fried onion flakes, bacon crumbles, and four types of salad dressing.

Every constituent of Chez August was present.

Timothy August—grandfather to Kix, owner of the house, elementary school principal, enough gray in his hair that he was considering dyeing it.

Sheriff Stackhouse—highest-ranking law enforcement officer in Roanoke, hard-ass, pretty green eyes, doted on Timothy and refused to let him use dye.

Nicole Beck—NSA analyst working with local U.S. Marshals office, partner to Manny, trim, sharp, and getting prettier by the day under the tutelage of her partner.

Plus me, Ronnie, Manny, GPA, and last but paramount, Kix.

Manny forced Noelle Beck to go first and he followed her down the counter, crafting their meals. Their completed salads looked remarkably similar as they sat at the dining table—steak with vinaigrette dressing.

Stackhouse and Timothy filled their plates next—chicken, cheddar, fried onions, tomatoes, and ranch dressing, both of them.

Ronnie and I diverged. I chose steak and blue cheese

dressing, lots of cheese and croutons. She chose chicken and bacon and veggies and vinaigrette.

From his high chair, Kix raised his juice cup and said, "CHEERS," a recent trick of his because of the overwhelming response he received. What could we do, not respond? We clinked our glasses with his and told him, "Cheers!" and he did it again, and we did it again, and when he did it a third time I told him to knock it off and leave his audience wanting more.

I asked the table to share about their day and focus on the eudaemonic, and Stackhouse said that wasn't a word, and Manny threw a crouton at me, and I lived in a house of Neanderthals, but they complied.

—*No students and no teachers at the elementary school today. Pure bliss.*

—*The whole department is undergoing a state audit. My deputies are working through their lunches and hating me for it, and I don't blame them.*

—*My afternoon clients canceled and I returned home to nap with Mackenzie. Unfortunately nothing R-rated happened.*

—*I made an old man cry and then I took a nap with a sun goddess. I tried something R-rated but she elbowed me in her sleep.*

—*I caught Melanie Vasquez at a 7-Eleven buying money orders with fake twenties,* la dama loca. *Had to process the paperwork myself because Beck's been on vacation with a known criminal kingpin.*

Beck set down her fork, wiped her mouth, and her cheeks were pink.

"Rocky Rickard proposed today," she said.

Manny sat straighter in his chair.

Stackhouse knocked her wine glass forward but caught it, sloshing a drop of cabernet.

"*Proposed*?" said Timothy August. He wiped his mouth too. "Congratulations. Was this expected?"

"It was not. At all."

"How exciting," said Ronnie. "Where? When? How?"

"*Cheers!*" said Kix.

Manny took a long drink on a bottle of low carb IPA. When he lowered it, the bottle make a soft sucking down. "Bought her a blood diamond with blood money, I bet."

Beck didn't look at him. "It's not a blood diamond, you dork."

"When?" said Ronnie.

"Today, before he left for Washington."

"Aren't we forgetting the most important part?" demanded Stackhouse. "What did you say, babe?"

She wasn't wearing an engagement ring, I observed. Like all things, I observed it well.

"I bet she said yes and now she's the new *Viuda Negra*, queen of the drug cartels," said Manny.

"Rocky has divested himself of all his illegal enterprises. He's sold numerous companies and informed his former colleagues that he's a legitimate businessman now," said Beck.

Manny made a snort.

"And he's not doing it solely for me," Beck continued. "He started the process before we met."

Stackhouse turned up her palm. "You said yes?"

"I... I didn't say anything. He told me not to."

"Details," said Ronnie. "I need details."

"I accompanied him to the airport." She smiled and only a fool would think Noelle Beck had anything but a charming smile. "He owns a private jet. A Cessna."

"Killed the former owner," said Manny.

"He did not. Anyway. He asked to show me the interior

of the jet. A table was set inside with champagne and the ring," she said.

"Oh my." Ronnie leaned backward in her chair and took a deep breath. "That's sexy as hell."

Stackhouse patted the table impatiently. "He told you not to respond?"

"He said I could leave with him right then. But if I wasn't ready, I should think it over. So I am."

"I'm surprised the *pendejo* didn't have you shot," said Manny.

"Good for you, babe." Stackhouse picked up her wine goblet and raised it to her. "You hooked a big one, and you're taking your time."

"Thank you." Her smile dimmed. "It's a lot. The whole thing, it's… It's a lot. I'm not thinking clearly."

Manny shook his head and make a tsk'ing noise. "Your mom's gonna have a fit."

"She's going to have two fits," said Beck.

"Cheers!"

"If you want to talk it over, I'll clear my schedule," said Ronnie.

Beck looked like a drowning woman being tossed a life preserver. "Yes please."

"Do you love him?" said Stackhouse.

"I don't *know*. No? Maybe? Isn't love supposed to be something you do, not only an emotion? If I say yes, then I'll begin to love him?" She shrugged and let the heaviness of it stoop her shoulders, and she pointed at Stackhouse and Timothy. "Why aren't you two married? When will you know it's time?"

The room jumped, like we'd been hit with a jolt of electricity.

Manny leaned away from Beck. "*Ay dios mio.*"

"Holy moly," I said.

*Something important was said, wasn't it. Some inner work-ings of adulthood that I don't understand? Can someone explain it? Or at least move us on to dessert?*

"Sorry, is that off limits?" Beck looked to us for help. "I feel like I walked into a mine field."

Stackhouse and Timothy grinned at each other, enjoying our discomfort, the villains.

"This is wonderful." Ronnie finished her wine and set it down, smiling. "I've wanted to ask that question for two years at least."

"There's no great secret to it, babe," said Stackhouse. "We're both happy with the way things are."

"But would marriage make us happier?" Timothy asked her.

"Maybe, maybe not," she said. "I feel oddly lucky and blessed to have this handsome man, and I'll take him as long as I can get him."

Ronnie took my hand and squeezed and it wasn't hard to guess what she was thinking.

Will marriage make one happier?

For me and Ronnie, yes.

For Charlotte Andrews and her husband? Maybe not?

For Beck and Rocky Rickard?

But was happiness even the goal?

"My looks are already fading," said Stackhouse. "And his perfect young teachers are looking more gorgeous by the day, I assume. They adore him like I do, so until a day comes that he wants to trade me in, I'll count my blessings."

"Your looks are not fading," said Timothy August. "I'm the lucky one. You are the catch."

She nudged him with a shoulder. "Aren't we maudlin and disgusting."

"Yes," I said. "Yes you are."

"I'm the best I've ever been when I'm with Timothy. He makes me a better person," Stackhouse told Beck. "If he ever proposes, I'll say yes. But we're old, babe. Don't use us for an example."

"He makes you a better person." Ronnie tilted her head back and spoke at the ceiling, mostly to herself. "That's it, isn't it. Making him better. Making me better. Or at least, that's a lot of it. But how do you explain that to someone who is self-centered."

"That self-centered comment better not be about me, *señorita*." Manny took his plate to the sink, food half finished. He washed the dish, his movements too loud and forceful. "Cause I'm feeling so generous I might walk Beck down the aisle."

"I didn't ask you to," she said.

"No man gets you unless I give you away, Beck."

"Of course Manny Martinez wants to be the focal point of someone else's wedding. Even mine," said Beck.

"Better not tell Rocky's guests I'm coming. None of them will show up."

"Maybe you won't receive an invitation."

"Gonna be embarrassing I arrest him at the altar," said Manny.

"He's not a..." Beck stood too and she turned her face to the front door. "It's been a long day, and I need to leave. Thank you for dinner."

She walked quickly to the front door, and it opened and closed on silken hinges. She was gone softly, as to not bother anyone.

Manny muttered something under his breath and he stomped up the rear staircase, both him and Beck leaving behind tomes of obvious and unspoken words.

"Shit," said Stackhouse and she sighed. "Those two."

*Did it happen again? It happened again, didn't it. Some adult thing that I can't see?*

"What fools we mortals be," I said. "And what tangled webs we weave."

Kix slammed his juice on the tray twice.

*You're quoting something but you botched it. This family is BARELY hanging on.*

## 13

A three-hour drive loomed before me, so I filled up at the Sheetz on Williamson—you will never find a more wretched hive of scum and industry—and purchased a coffee and two packs of trail mix, the kind with M&Ms because life is good. I drove to Interstate 81, and I set the cruise control on seventy-five and motored into the mountains near the borders of North Carolina and Kentucky.

Coal country. An enormous swath of land that oppressed my spirit—the coal factories were abandoned as demand dropped, and the terrain was too mountainous to sustain large farms, leaving behind skeletal towns of people who didn't know where to go.

One such town was Big Stone Gap. As coal sagged, so had the town's prospects. For a while it was known only as the place where actress Elizabeth Taylor nearly died choking on a chicken bone, as she campaigned with her husband John Warner. However, in 1999, the Commonwealth of Virginia built Wallens Ridge Prison on the outskirts of the town, providing millions for the local economy, and thus was the town allowed to endure, and from whence Caleb James had escaped earlier this year.

He was the only man to successfully break out of Wallens Ridge. Proof enough that Caleb was no fool.

As the hills fled by, I couldn't shake the image of Caleb's poor father, alone on the side of a mountain, sitting on his front porch... with a child's play set in his backyard. Did Caleb father a child? It'd never been mentioned in court records—I checked. Is that why he risked a jailbreak? To be with his kid? One of these days I'd have to grill Caleb's father about it, and make him cry again, even though I knew beforehand he'd lie to me, whatever the truth was. I brokered pain for facts, except they weren't facts.

Mackenzie August—master of his stupid dumbass horrible profession.

THE WARDEN of Wallens Ridge Prison shook my hand and regarded me from behind his desk with the same defenses he regarded all creatures big and small. The defense felt professional and efficient, not mean. Necessary to survive. His desk was bolted to the floor and the name plaque on it read Warden Brooks. My chair was bolted down too. Behind him, through the security window, Appalachian mountains rose in green glory.

He was a thick and squat man, plain like a prison door, with short curly dark hair. I'd interrupted his lunch. His Stanley Classic thermos steamed with coffee and his home-made sandwich was only partially unwrapped. Looked like ham and cheese. Next to his lunch sat my credentials.

"With no disparagement intended toward your profession," said Warden Brooks, "what chance does a private cop have of finding something that I didn't? Or that the federal marshals missed?"

"Sometimes what's needed is a fresh pair of eyes," I said. "I got the freshest around."

He made a grunting noise and he spoke with a southern accent, not like a plantation-owning gentleman but a man whose ancestors worked farms but never owned them. "I'm out of the loop now. You boys any closer to catching Mr. James?"

"Hope springs eternal."

"Other than that?"

"There are no leads to speak of. Embarrassing, isn't it," I said.

"Not embarrassing. Man broke out of a supermax. That's saying a lot." Warden Brooks drummed his thick fingers on his desk. "I don't see the harm in you looking at the videos. But believe me, we searched them good. However he got out, Mr. James had an intimate under-standing of our surveillance dead zones. You won't find a thing."

"I'm not interested in how he got out. I'm after relation-ships." Somewhere inside the concrete fortress, a series of doors slammed in concert. Echoes of the impact reached us, and I felt it in my feet. Eight hundred violent men were kept in cages nearby.

"Explain that to me," he said.

"It's a big world. I can't go knocking door-to-door. Marshals are better at that anyway. There's a small chance someone here knows something, and there's an even smaller chance that person will divulge it to me, rather than a mean guy with a badge. I make a career out of chasing small chances."

"Tough way to scratch a living."

"Through painful toil will I eat food from the cursed ground all the days of my life," I said.

His eyebrows, which needed a trim, pushed together to make a furrow in his forehead. "Hell's that mean?"

"Merely quoting the word of God."

"You're kind of a smart ass, aren't you," he said but he said it in a way that was disarming, like we might still be friends. "Sit tight." He took my credentials and left the room and presumably made a phone call. I spent the time picturing Ronnie at church. She always caused a stir there. The other parishioners didn't act normal around Ronnie; they *pretended* to act normal, the same way drivers pretend to act normal near a cop. It's a show of normalcy that uses up a lot of calories. She said she might go today without me, something she'd never done, and I wondered if there'd be a revival in the congregation.

Warden Brooks returned and said, "Some folks in Roanoke hold you in high regard, Mr. August."

"Odd, isn't it."

He consulted a chart on his desk. Mumbled something about it being a Sunday morning and chapel finishing, and he flipped up a page and consulted further. He nodded to himself and reached for his landline. Into the receiver he said, "Call Allan Johnston, please. My office. Thank you." He returned the phone to its cradle. Took a breath. "Caleb James. Man became the jailhouse investor. Skinny guy like him needed a way to survive in prison, so he gave out financial advice. I'm told he pushed cryptocurrency at the right time, and advised selling it before the crash in '21. He helped a handful of guys double their money, and soon the goons were arranging meetings with him at the library and then making phone calls to move their money around, if they had any. Course, I found this out after the fact. Caleb kept to himself and didn't make friends, outside of that."

Allan Johnston arrived, a deputy warden. Where Brooks was short and thick, Johnston was tall and boney and his head was shaved. His eyes were dark and deep like coal pits.

"Johnston, this's a private cop named August, looking into Caleb James. Escort him to the library, would you, and when he's done escort him to the parking lot. It's a waste of his time and ours but let's be polite about the thing."

Allan Johnston nodded.

I thanked Warden Brooks and he returned to his lunch as I walked with Johnston out of the office. Johnston found release forms for me to sign, and a guy at a security window accepted my wallet, phone and keys for safe-keeping, and Johnston patted me down and walked me deeper into the prison. Our route took us outside, across a stifling hot yard, to a different building. The prison felt alien, a remote planet of concrete and metal. Encircled by double layers of security fencing with razor wire. Two armed guards patrolled the roof of each cell block and the central structures.

How could a man slip out of here alive? And then out of Big Stone Gap undetected?

"Did you know Caleb James?" I said.

"No." Deputy Johnson was as tall as me and he walked faster.

"Any guess how he escaped?"

"Don't care."

"Did you know Virginia has one of the lowest recidivism rates in the country?" I waited. "Are you not bursting with pride?"

"How about you," he said, "do what you gotta do and don't talk to me and then get out of this little hell of ours before you get hurt."

"Ever read Jane Austen?" I said.

He did not reply. Which, I thought, was telling.

The prison library consisted of ten long rows of head-high bookshelves, six computer terminals, three conference tables, and a circulation desk. The shelves held fiction, non-fiction, and reference books. I knew a patron would find no homoerotic material and no books that would enflame interracial hostilities, but lots of material on abuse, which was believed to help prisoners learn about themselves. The place was utilitarian and metal and ugly, as were all things designed to be easily scrubbed of fluid.

Six inmates were browsing the shelves, two sat at a table with a small stack of law books, and one guy manned the circulation desk. All of them were black and wore an orange jumpsuit.

Johnston did his best to loom over me and look intimidating. "Wallens doesn't have a librarian right now. It's inmate-operated until we do. You follow? You ask your questions and don't make anyone angry and you push that alarm button in an emergency, but August, there better not be an emergency. You follow that."

"Where's the librarian?"

"I told you. Wallens doesn't have one."

"I mean, where'd he go?" I said.

"Greener pastures. You know how many candidates with a degree in library science want to move to Big Stone Gap and work at the prison for a tiny fucking salary? Not a damn one." He spoke over my shoulder. "Mason, help this guy out, he gets in trouble."

Mason, the large man at the circulation desk, threw Johnston a nod. "Got it, bossman."

Johnston left me in the library with nine prisoners and no guards. Maybe I should tell them I'd recently spent four whole nights in jail, wrongfully charged. That I was one of them.

"Long way from home, bigman," said Mason. He smiled and he had dimples, and one of his eyes pulled toward the middle.

"You don't think I fit in?"

"Know a cop when I see one. How much you want for them Nikes?"

"What do you have to trade?" I said.

"Can get you pills. Don't know what kind though, till you pop them. New razor. Cherry hooch. Some badass hooch now."

"Did you know Caleb James?"

Mason shook his head. He was leisurely working through a stack of books and shooting them with a laser gun and the computer beneath the desk would beep.

"Don't know no Caleb James."

"Skinny white guy who broke free. Used to dole out financial advice here," I said.

"You talking about Wall Street. Yeah I knew Wall Street. Motherfucker tole me to buy Ethereum and you know what happened?"

"The economy tanked."

"Lost my ass. Two hundred dollars," said Mason.

"That's it? Lucky bastard."

Mason grinned. "All I had, though. Wall Street's still aight with me. He tole me to sell, actually, and I didn't cause it kept going up and up. Damn, that shit gets me."

I sat at the circulation desk next to him. The swivel chair threatened to shatter.

"How'd he get out?" I said.

"Shit, you think I know? You think I know how his ass got out but I'm still sitting here?"

One of the guys who'd been browsing the shelves came with two books—both by Robert Greene. He set the books on the ledge and punched a number into the keypad. Mason used his laser gun to scan the barcode on the back covers.

The guy was skinny. His face held no less than a dozen tattoos, small designs I didn't recognize. His right hand only had one finger, the thumb, but he scooped the two books with it.

The skinny, tattooed guy said, "White boy thinks Mason gone snitch on Wall Street and get his ass beat," and he laughed like a hyena.

"Who gone do it, Birdman? You? Like to see you try, fool. You know what I like about that one?" Mason nodded his head at the books the skinny guy held. "Chapters about seduction. I get out, got me a whole bag of tricks. Also the thing about, make the brother come to you so you establish who's boss."

Skinny guy, Birdman, shrugged. "Don't know the fuck you talking."

"You will."

"Yeah, well. Don't tell the white boy a got'damn thing."

"You think I'm telling his ass anything? First off, I don't know shit," said Mason.

"Yeah well."

"You knew Wall Street?" I said. "He lose you a bunch of money too?"

"Shut up whitey 'fore I make you eat this book," said Birdman.

Mason laughed, big dimples and his eyes disappearing. "Birdman, look at this white dude, his ass three times bigger'n yours. This a big white dude. He eat your ass whole."

"I wouldn't enjoy it, though. I'm a civilized big white dude," I said.

"Yeah well."

The skinny, tattooed guy named Birdman left.

Thus it went for the next four hours. I sat behind the desk and chatted with Mason about everything—he had two kids but they were too young to visit him, and he'd be out in nine years on good behavior, and he hadn't meant to shoot that bitch and he heard she regained the use of her right arm which meant his sentence should be reduced, and he was training to be a welder, and he still hoped to be one when he got out because the money was good and he liked physical labor—and I asked all inmates who visited the prison about Caleb James and his escape and I was told to shut the hell up, and Mason assured them each he was no snitch either.

A fruitless and frustrating afternoon. I'd missed lunch and my stomach growled. Mason was brought a tray for dinner at four, and he kicked everyone out at five. Time to lock up, and me stupider than I'd arrived.

I stepped out of my Nikes and set them on the circulation desk. Low-cut blue and gray Air Max.

"Just me and you here, Mason. Tell me something I don't know, and I'm gone."

Mason was six inches shorter than me but we probably weighed the same. I wondered where he got all the calories in here. He picked up my shoe and turned it over and said, "Damn, bigman. Good looking and clean. I get them taken away in a few days, but damn."

"Did you know the previous librarian?"

"Limpdick."

I grinned. "Yeah?"

"Called him Limpdick. Dunno why," said Mason.

"Where'd he go?"

"You think guards tell me shit?"

"He quit? Fired? Transferred?" I said.

"I don't know."

"Was he friends with Wall Street?" I said.

"We all friends with Wall Street." He set the shoe down. "You want me tell you one thing you don't know? Aight, here it is, bigman. Wall Street ain't do shit."

"How so?"

"*How so.* Who say *how so.* I mean, skinny little white guy Wall Street was innocent. You know how us inmates in here are innocent? Each one of us innocent? We ain't really, but Wall Street was. You can tell who is and who isn't. Wall Street was in for shooting a cop? Ain't no way, bigman. Ain't no way," said Mason.

"He was high on meth."

"So? I been high and I ain't shoot a cop."

"There's video of it," I said.

"I believe that shit when I see it."

Johnston walked me back to the security window, where I reclaimed my wallet, phone, and keys.

"Is Warden Brooks around?" I said.

"Already gone home." Johnston looked impatient for me to get the hell out of his prison.

"When did Limpdick quit?" I said.

"Say that again?"

"The librarian. They called him Limpdick. When'd he quit?"

"Don't remember." Johnston stopped at the security

door which led to the graceless foyer and the shining parking lot outside. "Don't care."

"What was his real name?"

"Don't remember that either. Kevin maybe."

"Kevin what?" I said.

"What'd I tell you? Don't know, don't care, get out."

"Johnston, want to step outside and see who's tougher? I'm willing to have a tough-guy contest. Pushups might be involved and luckily for you there's no math."

He leaned close enough I could smell tobacco on his breath. "You know why I act tough?" He inclined his head backward, indicating the guard behind the security window, and another armed guy watching from the inner door. Pale blue short-sleeve shirts with black patches, radios, jackboots. Neither guard looked like a Mackenzie-fan. "I got friends. You know why you act tough? Cause you're stupid and you're a jackass."

The door closed behind me harder than necessary and outside I told the parking lot, "That feels truer than I wish it was."

I walked to my car gingerly in plastic shower shoes one size too small.

## 14

I drove into town and parked at Curklin's, a local restaurant and bar. Downtown Big Stone Gap was crowded with pickup trucks and battered SUVs. Across the street from Curklin's was a long strip of storefronts that fifty years ago sold textiles, now converted into a coffee shop, electronics store, a florist, and a cuisine kitchen, all locally owned, no chains. Down the street I saw a bakery, another coffee shop, and a pizza joint, old construction but updated. The town was a redoubt of comfort for the hardworking men and women surrounding it.

Curklin's was a sports bar with ancient walls and new paint, bright steel stools, and big televisions. I sat at the bar with other large men and asked for whatever pilsner they had on tap, so the large men wouldn't think me delicate.

The bartender looked like she'd been prom queen as recently as five years ago and the energy and smile hadn't worn away yet. She called me stranger and took my order— waffle fries with powdered sugar and marshmallows to start (I KNOW, but the guy next to me had them and oh my gosh), and a chicken/lettuce/tomato/ranch wrap, plus another beer.

On the giant television, the Braves were warming up for the seven o'clock game against the Mets.

The big guy to my left elbowed me and I half fell over.

"Those are real," he said.

"Your elbow?"

"The waitress, Madison. They're real. You believe that? Everybody new asks so I figure I save you the trouble. They aren't fake," he said.

Madison looked born for seedier professions than serving drinks. She wore a deep scoop neck, like her figure wasn't more trouble than it was worth yet, but how long could that last. The guys at the bar watched her instead of the television and when I realized I was doing the same I looked away.

"What do you do?" I said.

"I run the dairy farm up Roundstone. The Thompson place. Been there twenty years," said the big man with the big elbow.

"So you're obsessed with milk production."

"Haha." He grinned at me and threw another elbow and I hated it. He was drunk. "That's good. Guess I am. Madison and the dairy farm. Obsessed with milk production."

Madison brought my appetizer from the kitchen. The sweet potato waffle fries hadn't taken long to cook, a bad sign, but with the sugar and marshmallow I could've been a kid at a fair and I ate them like one.

She came back and said, "Wow, someone liked the fries," and the guy next to me asked for another Jack and Coke, and she said, "Alright, Roddy, but you know the rule. This's the last one, you hear? I'm cutting you off."

Roddy grinned and asked her to come over when she got

off work and he'd make the drinks then, and she rolled her eyes and said, "Roddy, hon, you're a mess," and she poured me another beer without asking.

"You know many prison guards?" I asked Roddy.

He did a shrugging motion, like he was hurt Madison turned him down again. "Sure. Everyone does. That's what we got here. A lot of prison guards. Not many girls. Not many girls like Madison."

"You know Allan Johnston?"

"Mean sumbitch, lives his cousins on Beaverdam Creek. I wouldn't tangle with them, don't care how big you are." Roddy spoke like a drunk who was excellent at hiding it. He drained half his final Jack and Coke. "The Johnston clan."

"What about the librarian?"

"Who?"

"Prison librarian. Nicknamed Limpdick." I felt ludicrous each time I said it. "Did you know him?"

He closed his eyes, like recollection was hard. "Think I'd remember that one." Finished the drink, spilling some down his chin. "Don't need this, don't need *her*. Don't need her or milk reduction, whatever you said, don't... Drink somewhere got'damn else."

He shoved away from the bar, the stool tipping but I caught it, and he walked out the door on heavy steps. Two families purposefully didn't look at him as he lumbered through.

Madison came for his empty glass. "That old cow turd didn't pay."

"I'll cover it," I said.

"That's okay, sweetie, he forgets. I'll make him pay next time before I pour his first drink. But that's a real kind thing to offer." A bell rang and she fetched my chicken wrap and said, "Enjoy, sweetie."

A twenty-five-year-old girl shouldn't be calling me sweetie. Using tricks like that would soon grind off the smile and energy. Or maybe I was becoming a curmudgeon. She was good for business, that was obvious. She and the waffle fries could sustain a bar for a decade.

She returned a few minutes later from the loud herd down the bar and filled my beer glass again and I said, "That's the last one."

"You bet." She smiled. "You're new at Wallens?"

"I wish. Seems like a sweetheart of a place."

She laughed.

I said, "I'm only here for the day."

"I thought to myself, that handsome guy has hair too nice for Wallens."

"I'm looking for someone. Maybe you know him? He used to work there. I don't know his real name, Kevin maybe. Nicknamed Limpdick."

"Oh my *God*, what an awful nickname."

"Isn't it," I said.

"No I don't know a Limpdick." She laughed more and gave me a silly face. "Luckily for me, huh."

"He was the librarian."

"Oh," she said. "*Oh!* You're talking about Softy."

"Softy."

"Yeah, Softy, he was the librarian. I forgot about him."

"Softy. Limpdick. This poor guy," I said.

"His name wasn't Kevin. It was Benjamin. Benjamin something. He was too good for this place, anyway. You know? He didn't come to the bar, he went to the coffee shops and the bakery." She leaned toward me over the bar top, and had Roddy still been here he would've elbowed me. "He was gay. Did you know that already?"

"I didn't."

"He was sweet to me. The nicest guy. But being gay here is hard. You know? Buncha old cow turds. Probably they saw him eating croissants at the bakery and gave him the bad nicknames."

A drunk bellowed at her and she left to attend to the sweaty rabble.

When she came back, my plate was empty and I had cash on the bar waiting. Fifty dollars too much.

"All done? Someone likes to clean his plate."

"Benjamin what? What was his last name?" I said.

She set both hands on my forearm, which rested on the bar, and she squeezed. "I don't know, I don't remember, sweetie. And I was you? I wouldn't go asking the guards here tonight."

"When did he quit?"

"Quit? I heard Softy got fired."

"Fired for what?" I said.

"I don't know, sweetie, I'm sorry."

"Stop calling me sweetie."

"*Oh.* Oh boy, are you touchy. I don't mean anything by it." She didn't let go of my arm.

"It demeans both of us, Madison. You do that to enough people for enough years, giving little bits of yourself away to men, even innocently, there'll be nothing left of you. It also insinuates I'm easily flattered, like a simpleton. How long ago was he fired?"

"Six months, maybe? Are you mad at me?"

"Around the time of the prison break? That's when Softy was fired?"

"Yeah." She smiled and released me. "Yeah, that sounds right, swee... That sounds right, mister."

"Where'd he go?" I said.

"How would I know that? Back to wherever he came from. A nicer place than here, I'll say that."

"Benjamin something."

"Benjamin the gay librarian named Softy," she said.

I stood. "Madison. Thank you for the help. Keep the change."

"Thank *you*, sweetie. And I'm calling you sweetie 'cause I wanna. Where'd you get that money?"

"If you want something different from this, move to Roanoke and call Ronnie Summers and she'll get you a job," I said.

"What? Hang on. Why?"

"Because Ronnie learned trading parts of yourself to men and hoping it'll work is a losing game," I said.

"What's wrong with this?" Madison indicated the bar.

"Nothing's wrong with this. But that..." I indicated the men watching us, watching her. "That's gonna get old, being the main attraction."

"Thanks, mister. You're the nicest guy. Like Softy was. What's your name?" she said.

"Remember—Roanoke and Ronnie Summers." I shot her with my finger, like the way a badass would in the 1980s, and I felt good about it, and I left.

## 15

Halfway home to Roanoke, and the headlights were smearing into a blur from light rain moving across the state, and because my concentration was fading in and out.

Waffle fries do not a healthy man make.

I called Ronnie and she answered and said, "Hello Mackenzie, my husband," and if the guys in Big Stone Gap could hear their names spoken from the lips of Veronica Summers they'd forget all about Madison and her scoop neck.

"I'm an hour away from you. But closing the distance."

"Good. You can rub my feet while I read depositions."

"Sounds hot," I said.

"I haven't had a pedicure in weeks. So no it won't be. But maybe I'll read them topless."

"Then you will not get much reading done," I said.

"I will resist you. Anticipation is half the fun, Mackenzie."

"How was church?"

"I sat with Courtney and Marcus, and she passed me notes."

"And the sermon?" I said.

"I'm positive there was one."

"What was it about?"

"Mmm, don't remember. Wait, yes I do, because Courtney drew a picture. A king went onto the roof to spy on a hot girl in a bath, which he should *not* have done, Mackenzie."

"What should he have done?" I said.

"He already had seven wives. He should have tended to them, I'm sure. They must be lonely."

"So King David should've cared for his wives. For their sake? Or for his own sake?"

"I don't know, Mackenzie, Courtney and I started playing dirty hangman then," she said. "Don't be mad. This is why I don't go when you're not here. Oh, and Marcus needs to meet with you."

"About what?"

"He did not disclose that," she said. "He said to save an evening for him soon."

"Probably to discuss our iniquitous Philistine wives."

"That sounds like a church joke I don't get, which makes you a religious bully, and shame on you."

My phone beeped. An incoming call.

"See you soon," I said.

"Hugs and kisses, Mackenzie."

I switched to the incoming call and a new, masculine voice said, "Mackenzie August?"

"That's me."

The guy took a deep breath, sounded like, and let it out slow and there was a moment of silence. Ahead, the interstate inclined downward, revealing two miles of red rear lights and across the dark median brighter oncoming traffic.

The voice spoke. "I hear you're searching for me, Mr. August, and I hear you're good at it."

Little hairs on the back of my neck stood.

"Caleb James," I said. My mind scrambled. "I am good at it. And I'm not convinced you're in Mexico."

"When you trace this call, you'll discover it was routed through a VPN on a burner phone, using a burner app, originating from a disingenuous location. Mexico is a big place. Good luck."

"Ervin Lane doesn't live in Mexico. You're not looking for him any longer?" I said.

A kind of unhappy snicker in my ear. "I never was."

"Caleb, I know he was drunk that night. The night of your arrest."

"A lot of people know Ervin was drunk," he said.

"Which gives us leverage, because the drunkenness is a trump card. If you're willing to turn yourself in, I can cut you a better deal. Your first lawyer failed. We can do better. Less jail time."

"How about no jail time," he said.

"You killed a cop, Caleb."

"No I didn't, Mr. August. At least, I don't think so."

"You pled guilty to it," I said.

"I shouldn't have."

"Why did you?"

"They coerced me," he said.

"Coerced you how?"

Caleb didn't respond.

Keep him talking, August, don't let him hang up.

"You and Ervin were childhood friends," I said.

"I had a lot of childhood friends. He was one of them. Had nothing to do with that night."

"How's the addiction?"

"Haven't touched it in years. Clean and healthy. Thanks for asking," he said.

"Kicking meth isn't easy."

"Prison forced a, ah, mandatory detox. And you can't get it where I am, down in Mexico. Or if you can, I'm not looking."

"Caleb, I don't care if you're guilty or innocent. The marshals will catch you. They're good at this, and I am too."

"Look, so, here's why I'm calling."

"Turn yourself in, Caleb. I got a big lead today."

"You have a job to do, I get it. Keep looking. Look all you want. Maybe you'll find me down here, maybe you won't. But. Do me a favor. Don't harass Ervin. Leave him alone. The guy lost his hand," he said.

"Tell me about the girl. Rumor is, you and Ervin both dated Robin Lucas."

He ignored me.

"That's what keeps me up at night, picturing sad, drunk Ervin with one hand. Don't make his life worse. He didn't deserve any of this," said Caleb.

"He was drunk on duty. And you told me you're innocent. Someone's guilty of Kim Harper's murder."

"That's true," he said. A long pause. I had pulled over to the side of the interstate so I could focus. When had I done that? He repeated, "That's true. I was high. That's the one thing of which I'm guilty."

"Caleb—"

"Catch me if you can, Mr. August. But don't drive that poor man to suicide."

"Caleb," I said. "Caleb, tell me about Robin. Caleb."

Caleb hung up.

## 16

Samantha Miller, wealthy socialite and Baptist philan-
thropist, returned to the austere offices of Investigator
August, Monday afternoon. She remained in tip-top shape
and she wore another bright dress, a baby doll cut, pale
pink. Samantha was too old to wear it, probably, but she
didn't look too old to wear it—her legs and shoes were still
good, her eyes still big and blue.

She did not arrive alone. With her came reinforcements,
two women. If Boonsboro Baptist had a Real Housewives
show, these would be the stars behind Samantha. Their
heels made them taller, their skin a fraction too tight and
shiny. All of them wore colors too bright, but too bright on
purpose, shades of spring.

Samantha introduced us.

Sandra had dark hair, cut in a bob that reached her
chin.

Cynthia's hair was blonde and fell in feather waves and
her lips were fake.

Samantha, Sandra, Cynthia. Each of them carried two
shopping bags from local boutiques. They looked at me like

their combined might made them invincible and they knew it and I knew it too.

"Ew," I said.

Samantha set her bags down and put her hands on her hips. She looked happy with my comment.

"Ew, Inspector?"

"Your faces. They're awful," I said.

All three women laughed. Not a cackle but close.

"We each had a chemical peel, bright and early. You should see us in a few days," said Samantha. Their faces looked as though they'd spent a day in blistering sunlight and were about to peel.

"A gentleman," said Sandra, the brunette, "isn't supposed to notice."

"A gentleman would be blind."

"We bought lingerie to make it up to our husbands," said Samantha, and she sat in my client chair.

"Anything to take the eyes south," I said.

"Where is your *darling* dog?"

"I didn't bring her. Good thing, she would've bitten you."

"Oh hush," said Samantha. "Cynthia and Sandra attend my Sunday School. They're sitting in on our meeting, as fellow stockholders." She patted the client chair next to her. I only had two. Her two sidekicks both perched on the one chair, knees together, backs straight, hands on their thighs, like attentive schoolgirls.

"This is invigorating," said Sandra. "I've never been in a private investigator's office before. It's all so clandestine and sexy."

"That's my new potpourri."

"It's working," she said.

"Have you had a productive week?" asked Samantha.

I waffled my hand.

"Perhaps industrious is a better term. I haven't produced much," I said.

"Inspector. I'm disappointed."

"Yes, me too," said Sandra and she pouted.

"I expected more from you," said Samantha.

"Oh pooh," I said.

"Tell us about your week."

"Please," I said.

"What?"

"Tell us about your week *please*," I said.

Samantha Miller cocked her head to the side, as though in challenge. "You work for me, Inspector."

"And you're supposed to have southern charm, Boons-boro Baptist."

She looked at her two friends who smiled and shrugged and Sandra the brunette said, "This is *so* exciting. Wait till the others hear about it."

"They won't believe how big and handsome he is. Even larger than his photos," said Cynthia, and she toyed with her hair. With her tight skin, and the big lips, and the puffy red splotches, she looked like a recovering victim of abuse.

"And even better mannered," I said.

"*Fine.*" Samantha made a show of rolling her eyes. "Tell us about your week, pretty please."

I did.

I told them about meeting the prosecutor, the chief, the defense attorney, and my suspicion the entire justice system in Lynchburg was covering up the fact that Ervin Lane had been drunk as a skunk at the time of the arrest. I told them I interviewed Caleb's father, and Ervin himself, and I visited the prison, and I finished the story with the coup de grâce— the phone call from Caleb himself. The women each made a Baptist gasp and leaned forward then.

"Unproductive?" said Samantha. "Mr. August, you are unfair to yourself. I believe you've done yourself proud."

I shrugged and I did it modestly, which was hard, because I'm so great.

"So where is he?" said Sandra the brunette.

"He's still *at large*," said Samantha. "He's on *the lam*."

"He claims he's in Mexico. And there's a chance he's telling the truth," I said. "In which case, we're out of luck."

"You can't find him there?" said Sandra and she pouted again, which might be cute if she didn't look like Halloween.

"I might. But I won't try."

"Why not?"

"Life's too short. And I'd miss the blonde whom I sleep with," I said.

"Oh my," said Sandra, and Cynthia touched her own blonde hair.

"Keep looking in America, please, Mr. August," said Samantha. She twisted in her seat to reach her shopping bags, from which she produced a black Gucci purse. She twitched a check from it and laid it on my desk. The check was blank and hopeful, like the women's eyes.

"I have a plan," I said.

Sandra and Cynthia sat straighter and Sandra said, "Oooo, I thought you would. Isn't this *fun*."

"Maybe I can convince Caleb to turn himself in for reduced jail time," I said.

Samantha Miller frowned. Or she looked like she was trying—nothing moved on her forehead.

"Reduced jail time? Should he not be penalized with extra, for escaping?"

"If we're smart, we won't arrogate that authority onto ourselves. We're not the judge."

"We won't what?" said Sandra the brunette.

"That night was hell. It's presumptuous of us to determine what his penalty should and shouldn't be."

"He killed a woman," said Samantha stiffly.

"And he's a Presbyterian," said Sandra, and she and Cynthia fell to laughing. Samantha did not partake.

"He killed a police officer. And he was high. But there's more to this I can't see yet. That night didn't go down the way we think it did," I said.

"I'm not paying you to get him free of judgment," said Samantha.

"You're paying me to find him. And this might work."

"I want his prison term increased, not decreased. Work towards that end," she said.

"That won't be up to you. Or me. If I don't cut a deal with him, it'll be out of my hands. And yours."

"Nothing is out of our hands, Inspector. With God, all things are possible," she said.

"You botched that verse."

Samantha Miller stood. "Keep looking, Mr. August. Show no mercy to that man."

"Ooo, we could help you look," said Sandra the brunette.

"No thank you."

"Why not?" Cynthia did her pout.

"I'd prefer the help of a spicy chicken sandwich."

"Don't be silly," said Sandra. "We're rich. We can do anything."

Jiminy Christmas.

## 17

After the triumvirate of Baptist glamor left, I made a phone call to human resources at the Virginia Department of Corrections. Who was the librarian at Wallens Ridge State Prison two years ago?

-One moment, sir, let me check... Benjamin Roy.

Perfect. And when did Benjamin Roy quit?

-Earlier this year, sir. February.

Where is his new place of employment?

-I don't know, sir.

Do you think he helped Caleb escape prison?

-I beg your pardon?

Nothing, goodbye.

I used my laptop as a Google machine and discovered a Benjamin Roy was currently the librarian at Averett University, a three-hour drive from Wallens Ridge, and a ninety minute drive from my office. What do you know about that.

DANVILLE SAT on the border of Virginia and North Carolina.

Like Big Stone Gap, it'd seen better days but Averett University helped. A small private college, leafy, white columns, brick. Only nine hundred undergraduate students, most home for the summer.

I parked in front of the Mary B. Blount Library and wandered in. Averett's endowment was only twenty million dollars (Harvard's endowment was forty-two billion, University of Pennsylvania's was fifteen billion, you get the idea), so the library was old and wouldn't be getting an upgrade soon, but the girl at the circulation desk smiled at me, and there were two students working at a table, and the place felt intimate and relational, like the librarians would help you research instead of merely directing you off into the caverns of books.

"I'd like to borrow *Fifty Shades of Grey*, please," I said.

The coed laughed. "You don't look like the type."

"I'm not. Not limber enough. I'm Mackenzie."

"Hi Mackenzie, I'm Dream. Can I help you?"

"Lies," I said.

"What?"

"What's your real name?"

She smiled brightly. "It's Dream. My mother's a pothead, but I like it. Don't you?"

"Pot? Not in a long time," I said.

Dream laughed. Ol' Mackenzie, still got it.

"Is Benjamin Roy in?"

"Absolutely! Come with me, Mackenzie," she said, and we walked behind the circulation desk, which would *never* happen at Harvard, to a corner office with tall windows overlooking a green lawn. A man sat at a desk, peering intently at his monitor, his left hand holding a hardback reference book open, his right hand on the computer mouse.

"Mr. Roy? Have a minute for a visitor?" she said.

"I do. Come in, please." Benjamin Roy closed the book and stood. He was on the short side, and everything about him was trim. His close-cropped hair, his wireframe glasses, his slim-fit pressed oxford shirt. Behind him was a framed Library Science diploma from George Mason. Other than that, the office wasn't personalized. Based on the timeline, he probably was hired last month.

Dream gestured for me to enter and I did and she left, and I said, "Benjamin Roy, I'm Mackenzie August."

"Have a seat, Mackenzie?"

I did. He did.

"What can I do for you?"

"I'm a man who chases coincidences, Benjamin. Because often they aren't. I'm chasing the coincidence that Caleb James frequented your library at Wallens—a prison where he had a good reputation, a prison you were far too kind and educated for, a prison he escaped from, which necessarily required an employee to facilitate, and a prison that fired you soon after."

As I talked he leaned away from me, like I might burn him, and the blood drained from his head, leaving his face pale and his neck splotchy.

"It isn't hard to put two and two together, Benjamin," I said.

"I don't have time for this... for this...absurd..."

"I'm sure you were investigated by Internal Affairs."

"Of course. Of *course* I was. And I was charged with nothing. There's no evidence I helped Caleb escape and I'll thank you very much to leave. Lord, I'm done with this narrative. I left it behind," said Benjamin.

"I went there. To your library at Wallens. Mason's running the show because they can't find a replacement."

Still in shock, he half smiled. "Mason is the correct choice. He's competent and he understands the importance of books to prevent mental atrophy and character decay."

"That prison felt rotten."

"It's a small bastion of hell, Mr. August."

"You didn't fit in there. That's what Madison said. At Curklin's bar."

"Madison." Another half smile. "She was a bright spot."

"She said you're too nice for the prison and for Big Stone Gap. That she didn't blame you for leaving, that it's hard to be gay there."

"I like southern towns, Mr. August, like Big Stone Gap and Danville. It was only the prison that I objected to. I grew up in Martinsville," he said.

"I'm sorry to hear that."

"I don't—"

"Here's what I want to do, Benjamin. I want for us to go for a walk. I leave my cell phone at the circulation desk, but you're welcome to take yours. I want you to hear my questions, and decide which to answer, and then if all goes well, I leave and you never see me again."

"Why the hell would I do that?" said Benjamin.

"Never seeing me again is a big plus. Especially at your new place of employment."

"Oh Lord." He stood. "Fine, let's get this over with."

"That's what my wife says too."

"I hope that's not true," said Benjamin.

"It's not. I'm dynamite. Let's go."

WE STROLLED down West Main Street and onto the Schoolfield House Courtyard. It was as you would picture it

—a green lawn surrounded by academic brick and trees and students on their phones, two guys lazily tossing a frisbee. It was hot and humid and most humanity was indoors.

"Why the hell did you take a prison job," I said.

"Naivety." Benjamin pronounced it NIGH-eve-eh-TAY. "And optimism. I could change the world, you know? Lord, did that wear off quick. It wasn't the inmates that got to me. It was the guards. Disgusting creations, and the nicknames they gave me? Some of the sentries are far worse than those they rule over. And I wasn't fired, by the way. I quit."

"If you hadn't quit, would they have fired you?"

"They threatened to. There's no proof against me—they even vacuumed my trunk for DNA—but their lawyer said they could force my termination through loopholes about safety and incompetence and trust, and if I quit then they'd drop me from their list of suspects. It might've been bluster, but I was happy to get the hell out of there with a clean resume." His hands were clasped behind his back as he walked. College suited Benjamin Roy better than a prison. "And for the record, the man you're searching for, Caleb James, he's innocent."

"How do you know?"

"Because I was with the man for hours, every day, for over a year. You get to know who a person is and who a person isn't under duress like prison," said Benjamin.

"Meth makes monsters out of men. The man you knew in prison is not the man who was pulled over that night."

"Meth makes monsters out of men. That's artful. Did you make it up?"

"I hope so. Tell everyone," I said. "Regardless, whoever helped Caleb escape has my admiration."

"Oh really." Benjamin suspected a trap but he would play along.

"In general, the world runs smoother if we all obey the rules. Like on a highway. But in Caleb's case, if you really believe an innocent man is incarcerated... Not many would risk their career and freedom to help him. It required a supernal moral compass and a Herculean set of balls."

We strolled quietly a moment.

"Would you have helped him?" said Benjamin.

"I doubt it. I'm too, ah, old and jaded now. Not romantic enough."

"He and I weren't romantic, if that's what you mean. Nor sexual."

"That isn't what I meant. Let's play a game. Me and you out here with no phones. A hypothetical game."

Benjamin chuckled.

"You want to know how Caleb got out, hypothetically. I'll tell you this. For the record, in case you're somehow recording this to get a confession, it *wasn't* me. But if it had been? What a fitting way for me to give the finger to that place, knowing I planned to quit soon after."

We stopped walking under the shade of a maple tree whose roots were threatening to break up the sidewalk.

"I don't care how he got out. I want to know where he was taken. If it had been you who helped him escape, hypothetically, where would you have driven him?" I said.

"If I helped Caleb escape, why would I tell you that? Obviously I would want him to remain free."

"Because you were being naive. As you said."

"You said I had a supernatural moral compass," he said.

"Supernal. It was naive to think he wouldn't be caught. He will be, and his sentence will be worse. I'm his only shot at getting lesser jail time, not more."

"How would you do that?" said Benjamin. We were close

in the shade, but he was watching the lawn, not me, his hands behind his back.

"I'll force Caleb into a plea deal. I uncovered information that'll help prove that night wasn't all his fault. He and I have spoken on the phone, and I bet we will again. If I can prove I'm getting closer, it'll force his hand."

"Mr. August, I don't know where Caleb is. And I'm not helping you."

"Mr. Roy. I'm his best shot."

"I'm sorry but I don't believe you."

"He'll be captured soon. That'll weigh heavily when you remember this conversation," I said.

"Hah. He's smarter than you think. And I'm not saying another word about this."

I nodded. "I figured you might not. Shucks."

"Are we done? I have work."

"Sure. I suppose I'll be early to my next appointment. Can you point me to Averett Central? It's next to the Main Hall," I said.

He pursed lips and looked at me for the first time in a while. "Your next appointment is in Averett Central?"

"With Dr. Richardson."

"The Vice President of the school? You're meeting with the Vice President? Why? Why her?" he said.

"Because I'm told the president, Dr. York, is on vacation in St. Simon."

Benjamin's voice had risen an octave. "Yes, but... Why meet with either? Are you blackmailing me?"

"Of course not, Benjamin. I'm looking for information. Sheesh."

"No no no," he said. "What information could Dr. Richardson possibly know about Caleb James' escape?"

I did a shrug. A natural, innocuous shrug, and it was supernal in its delivery.

"Maybe you confided in her about your involvement in his jailbreak."

"You're going to ask Dr. Richardson..." Another octave and a few extra decibels from Benjamin. "You think I would've... Of *course* I didn't confide in her!"

"Maybe, maybe not. I'll find out."

"That's bullshit! This is blackmail!"

"Calm down, Benji. Working at Wallens should've made you unflappable. But here you are, flapping." I turned and pointed at the largest building. "That's gotta be the Main Hall."

His arms were no longer clasped behind his back. They were crossed over his chest and he was glaring. Quite undignified for a dignified librarian.

"Bullshit, you're bluffing. You don't really have an appointment with Dr. Richardson."

"Yes, Benjamin Roy, I do. In twenty minutes.

In fact I did not have one. I was being a liar.

"Mr. August. Please. *Please* don't do this," he said. "I'm a new hire. You cannot, you simply *cannot* run to my supervisor's supervisor and tell her I helped a convict escape earlier this year."

"Because you didn't help him," I said.

"That's right!"

"But if you had. Hypothetically. Would you have smuggled him out in your car? And where would you have dropped him off?"

Benjamin did an eye roll. A huge one.

"You're sweating," I said. "Is it the heat? We can walk to the Main Hall together, get into some air conditioning."

"Lord, you think you're hilarious."

"Wrong. I am hilarious. Was Dr. Richardson an accomplice? Is that what you're insinuating?" I said.

"Why don't you go to hell."

"Wait until she hears you implicated her. Have a good day, Mr. Roy." I turned to go.

"Wait." He grabbed at my arm. "Wait, you asshole. Wait."

I gave him a moment.

And I said, "They'll catch him, Benjamin."

"I swear to God I don't know where Caleb was going. Or where he is now."

"I believe you."

"Hypothetically," he said and he did another expansive eye roll and stared upward into the green maple leaves, so bright in the sunlight they could be glowing. "Hypothetically. Caleb didn't deserve to be in prison and whoever helped him escape deserves a fucking medal. If it was me, and it *wasn't*, but if it was me then I would've driven him wherever he asked."

"Where was that?"

"I imagine he would've asked to go home. To Lynchburg."

"Where in Lynchburg?" I said.

"I don't know. Maybe behind a Sheetz gas station or something. Hard to say, Mr. August."

"A Sheetz."

"Yes. Hypothetically. It's possible, who knows."

"Did anyone meet Caleb at the Sheetz?"

"I have no idea." Benjamin shrugged at me like an angry teenager.

"Did he have a phone? Hypothetically."

"Not to my knowledge."

"Was Robin rendezvousing with him?"

"Maybe. I don't know if she was or not."

"He told you about Robin."

"Lord, of course he did. The man was in prison, what else is he supposed to talk about?" said Benjamin.

"What about her?"

He looked at me and through me and his eyes drifted upward, to his left, to the memory quadrant. He thought a moment. "He loved her. He screwed it up, but she'd forgiven him. Something like that."

"Who else did he mention?"

"The bastard who pulled him over. Boy did he hate that man. I don't remember his name."

"What did Caleb say happened that night?" I said.

"I never asked. I don't know. But whatever it was, Caleb isn't a murderer."

"Did Caleb have a kid?"

"Yes, of course. A son."

He did! Holy smokes. Nobody knew anything about a kid. I played it cool.

"What'd he say about his kid?"

"That he couldn't wait to meet him. That he would set up a retirement account for him and all that. That he needed to get the hell out of prison," said Benjamin.

"You didn't worry, once caught, Caleb would roll over on you?"

"See, this proves you don't know Caleb. He wouldn't. He was a good man," said Benjamin.

"Where was he going?"

"I told you. I have no idea where he was going. Or who was meeting him. Or what his plans were. Hypothetically, you big asshole, I parked my car behind a Sheetz, popped the lock on my trunk, walked inside to use the restroom and get a coffee, came out, closed my trunk, and kept driving."

"And later vacuumed your trunk."

"Vacuumed the hell out of it three times," said Benjamin.

I nodded to myself and decided I'd pushed him enough. Maybe there was more, maybe there wasn't. If it was still possible, I'd like to leave Benjamin with us on good terms, so the well could be plumbed again.

"Thank you, Benjamin. I'll go."

"It's about damn time," he said.

"If there's anything else you know, better tell me now, to reduce the chance of me returning."

"I know he was innocent. I know I'm glad he's out. I hope he's with his son, and I pray you never find him," said Benjamin.

"At least we're parting on good terms."

"Like hell we are," said Benjamin and he turned on his heel and marched away.

I DROVE ten miles over on the way home, wild man, so I'd have time to take Kix to the playground before dinner. And because I was engorged with life, new leads, new facts, the splendor of work paying off.

While in prison, Caleb had spoken often of Robin, and of his son.

His son!

When had Caleb discovered Robin was pregnant? Before that night? While in jail, awaiting his trial? Had Ervin Lane known about the son? How recently had Ervin been dating Robin before she was knocked up by Caleb?

This mattered for two reasons.

One, it might be additional leverage to force both sides into a plea deal. A good lawyer could make it look like drunken Ervin had been harassing Caleb, especially in light of the romantic triangle.

Two, it might be a titanic step closer to finding Caleb. Find Robin, find his son, find the man.

I checked my phone as I drove on a mostly deserted Martinsville Highway. I'd missed a phone call from an unknown number, but a voicemail had been left.

*August, this is Police Chief Jake Robertson. Listen, go on and give me a call back because you and I need to get a few things straight. I'll tell you right now I am not happy. I come into the office this Monday morning and find out you visited Ervin out west last Friday, after I plainly told you not to. I don't take it well at all, you coming to me for help and then bothering that ol' boy against my wishes, no sir I do not. I told you once, you investigate that sum'bitch Caleb James all you want, and I hope to hell you find him, but you leave Ervin out of this. No actually, while I'm saying this, I'm getting madder than hell and I'm changing my mind. I don't want you investigating Caleb James. At all. You hear? Your investigation is concluded as of right now, I don't care what Samantha Miller says or how much she paid you, I'll arrest you both for interfering in an investigation. We'll find that runaway. Not you. You take exception with anything I just told you, call me and I'll chew your ass right off.*

Click.

If Robertson had called from a landline, I bet he slammed the receiver then. If he'd called from a cell phone, I bet he wished he'd called from a landline, cause pushing the END button wasn't as satisfying.

Little of what he threatened was legal. He didn't have a say-so in my arrangement with Samantha Miller. He couldn't stop me from investigating Caleb. And if he tried to chew my ass off, I could hang up on him, satisfying no matter how I did it.

Did this constitute new information?

Ervin wanted to be left alone. And he asked me to stop looking for Caleb.

Caleb wanted to be left alone. And he asked me to not hassle Ervin.

The chief demanded I stop my investigation of both men.

Benjamin Roy wanted me to leave Caleb alone. So did Caleb's father.

Nobody wanted me to do the things I was doing, except Samantha Miller, but she didn't approve of my current plan.

It seemed no persons were happy with me. Despite the fact I was doing the things so well, with verve and élan and panache. No one ever mentioned my panache.

## 18

That night Ronnie and I sat on our front porch swing with margaritas. We were hot but a good hot. A consistent July breeze blew the humidity down the street, so it wouldn't settle in, and mosquitos were driven off by two citronella incense sticks, the smoke swirling around us before wafting away in the breeze. John Coltrane played softly on the speaker. In a sentimental mood, Ronnie and I hadn't spoken in fifteen minutes. Proximity was enough.

She was reclined sideways so her feet were in my lap. She hadn't changed her outfit since coming home late from her office, but she'd kicked off the heels, removed the white leather Valentino belt, and loosened and unbuttoned the pink shirt. Her eyes were closed, her head tilted against a pillow propped on the chain, and she was smiling. One bead of perspiration trickled down her neck from the warmth created by the pillow and her hair. The drop sped quickly along her collar bone before pausing in the hollow of her throat. She sighed and shifted and the small drop jostled and continued down her chest but lost speed when forced to climb one of the curves of her body created by her white brassiere. And yet, as I watched... yes, here it goes... slowly it worked sideways instead of forward, toward the valley of hot skin, maybe accelerated by the lubricant of humidity. On the crest of the curve, perhaps catching a microscopic imperfection of the skin, the droplet perched, glowing, reflecting a point of light...... at last, spilling... the bead of moisture plummeted, gone, out of sight behind the folds of her shirt and bra, but I felt satisfied, though already hoping for another.

"Mackenzie," she said.

"Yes Ronnie."

"Isn't it nice when the alcohol hits your brain."

"You've only had half of one margarita."

"Yes but it entered my bloodstream and I felt it move around, like a chill, and I paid attention when the effects reached my brain. And it was like..." Eyes still closed, she smiled wider. "...like, *ahhhh*."

"That smile could launch a thousand bottles of tequila."

A car turned onto our street, Windsor, headlights illuminating our trees from a new direction. A big Lexus LS and it braked at our curb. The engine died and Marcus Morgan stood out of it. For a moment he remained at his car, looking up the street and down, the only man moving, partially highlighted by the lamp.

He walked up our sidewalk and he said, "Like my street better. But yours is close."

"My street has no drug lords," I said.

"There's that."

As usual, Marcus wore black slacks and a black shirt, button-up, short-sleeved, and a silver watch and silver ring and silver belt buckle. Today he wore a silver fine chain necklace. The slacks were pressed, and the shirt had little vertical stripes, making the tall man look taller.

"You want a margarita?" I said.

"Hell yeah I want a margarita. You think a man don't want a margarita cause he's Black?"

"It occurred to me."

"That's called prejudice, wonderbread."

"I'll get it," said Ronnie and she stood before I could. "I am the hostess with the most."

Marcus thanked her and sat on the rocking chair opposite me, and he said, "Should make you get it, teach you a lesson about interracial relations."

"I know all about interracial relations. I know Black people and Mexicans are crazy racist toward the other, but the media ignores it because that doesn't outrage White people, which is what's required to keep cable news channels in business."

Marcus grinned. "You listened. Sometimes I wonder."

Ronnie returned with a pitcher and an empty glass. She filled his, the icy mixture more melted than it had been, and refilled my glass. "Do you boys need to be alone while you determine the fate of the world?"

"No, please join," I said.

She sat and raised her half empty glass. "Cheers to beautiful men."

"Cheers to you and wonderbread," said Marcus.

"Cheers to you and *moyo*."

Marcus grinned. "Call me *moyo* all you want. I like it, cause we cool. But I wouldn't use it next time you in a hiphop club."

"Is it offensive?"

"To the weak-minded and the low self-esteemed."

Ronnie curled up with her feet under her and she drank some margarita.

"How long have you and Courtney been married, Marcus?"

"Twenty years."

"And you're happy? She's happy?" said Ronnie.

"I'm happy. Happy as can be married to crazy. She's... She's mostly happy."

"Only mostly?"

Marcus kinda shifted his shoulders, like working something loose.

"You live with a woman like Courtney long enough, you start to wonder if she ain't never gonna be completely happy. Like something inside her is broken and she's mad at you cause you haven't fixed it yet. Sometimes when I feel philosophical, I wonder if a woman like Courtney, if her life's work isn't to realize that, figure that shit out every day, that she's in charge of her own contentment. And a man like me, his job is every day to understand he ain't all that important, that he's built to be a workhorse and anything else makes him restless."

"Good grief," I said.

"Getting closer to fifty, I'm doing some deep work on my own mortality. Ron, she asked the right question at the right time." Marcus drained most of his glass then in three large gulps, like he still had deep work to do. "Are you two happy?"

She nodded.

"Yes. I am. But perhaps I'm a woman like Courtney. Now that I've been married a while, I'm becoming aware that... It's hard to put into words. That if any man on earth has what it takes to complete me, it's him, this superman of a husband, but I don't know if he can."

"Good thing to realize," said Marcus.

"She's doing some divorce work she doesn't want to do. And it's turning the screws on her," I said.

"Ah. Tough way to make a living."

"And dealing cocaine is a pleasure cruise?"

"I don't deal. I maintain relationships and a happy work environment, fool," said Marcus.

Ronnie rejoined.

"If no man is capable of making me feel complete, then that means the problem is internal. The problem is me. Now my childhood friend wants a divorce and I'm looking at her... like I could be looking at myself... and I know what she's feeling, that something's wrong, but she's running the wrong direction. But do I know what the right direction is? Do I know..." She stopped and lost her steam and she took my hand. "I'm learning these wounds inside us are more irreparable than I thought when I was younger."

The coda to her thesis was so profound, so true on physical and spiritual levels, so close to uttering magic and creation, that I thought the earth around us hushed a moment as though a lion had strolled though.

I cleared my throat.

Marcus said, "Being a parent helps. But not all the way."

Ronnie smiled and nodded. She looked at me and then at him and she laughed, her music lightening the mood.

"Sorry. I didn't mean to depress the evening. Let's change the subject. Do you two need to discuss shooting an enemy or something?"

"Yeah something like that." He leaned forward in his chair to reach his back pocket.

"So predictable, you two," said Ronnie.

"I don't shoot people," I said. "My hands are remarkably clean, all things considered."

"Cause you getting lazy." Marcus held in his hand what

looked like an expensive jewelry case, big enough to hold a bracelet or small necklace. He tossed it to me. Covered with felt, the box was sturdy and strong, and I opened it. Inside were five rows of five diamonds, held in place and sparkling at me. Ronnie made a gasp. But they weren't diamonds, they were too large, and looking through them you could see they were red-tipped.

"Aurum," I said.

"Underworld currency. That's a lot. Darren never had that many," said Ronnie.

"Darren was small potatoes." He smiled. "By comparison to a player such as myself."

"Why're you showing me these?" I said.

"They're yours now."

"I don't want them."

"Too late. Already made it official. We more or less keep track in a ledger. Only so many aurum in the world. Keeping track makes it harder to steal them. Little chip inside the red dots. You having those makes you more safe, babe, not less safe."

"I'm already safe as heck," I said. "Aren't I?"

"It ain't you that's at issue."

"You're in danger."

He leaned backward in the chair and shifted his shoulders again.

"New man in town. We, ahh, butting heads."

"A District King?" said Ronnie.

"Call him a private consultant at the moment. But the man wants my job. Name's Doyle."

"Doyle." I snapped closed the case of criminal currency. "I know that name Doyle. Detective Green says he took orders from him. When I was framed for the murder of Maddie and the other guys."

"Why does Doyle hate Mackenzie?" asked Ronnie.

"He don't. Meg hated Mackenzie, when she framed him. Doyle only helped," said Marcus.

"You believe your life is in danger?" said Ronnie.

"Believe so."

"How does giving Mackenzie the aurum help?"

"If I'm gone, it provides you some protection."

I waggled this jewelry case. "Is this everything?"

"Naw, keeping some for myself. If Doyle's smart, and I think he is, he kills me he won't keep my aurum. He'll submit them back to the ledger."

"Murder is okay, but stealing aurum isn't?" said Ronnie.

Marcus raised his fingers, like—*who knows*.

"Ain't my rules, Ron." He nodded at the case. "They's a phone number inside. Puts you in contact with some folk who can help you use them, you ever need. Being honest, though, your amigo Manuel could help too. I figure that case goes to all three of you."

"You let it be known that you're giving me the aurum," I said.

"Indeed I did."

"That will make Doyle think twice. Because he knows I could cash them in and have him killed? For vengeance?"

"The thought occurred to me. Giving you that, s'good for you and s'good for me."

"I had hoped I was rid of this world," she said.

"Like the Israelites, you may have left Egypt but Egypt still be inside you."

"What," said Ronnie, "the hell does that mean."

"Moses freed his people from Pharaoh. But the people still had the mentality of slaves, although they no longer were," I said.

"That has nothing to do with me. Does it?"

Marcus grinned and stood. "Told Courtney, she gotta quit distracting you at church."

"How dare you," said Ronnie.

Marcus drained the last drop from his glass and set it down. "Hit the spot."

"Can you feel it in your brain?"

"Yes indeed."

"No you can't," I said.

"And everywhere else too. Y'all have a good night," he said.

"What if I throw this box away?" I called.

"Then you a bigger dumbass than you look."

BEFORE BED I let Georgina Princess August into the backyard, where she sniffed and did her business. I checked every door to ensure they were locked. Looked in on Kix—he was sleeping soundly. Looked in on Manny—he was out, lost in the night, revoking the freedom of the wicked. Brushed my teeth. Flossed. Gargled with mouthwash. And wondered why Ronnie's nighttime bed-prepping process lasted so much longer than mine.

She was in bed and I gleaned through minuscule behavioral subtleties that she was too tired and distracted for romance, and so it was with a normal, steady heartbeat that I got into bed beside her.

"Are you worried?" she said.

"About Marcus. No."

"Why not?"

"It's out of my control. I try not to worry about things over which I have no input," I said.

"That's fine. But I'm not asking what mental activity

you'll allow yourself. I'm asking about your emotional state."

"To me they're closely related. But here's a more thorough account of my emotional state..." I reclined against my pillow—goose down with a silk cover because my wife was extra—and gazed at the ceiling. "This new guy, Doyle, seems to be a player to take seriously, but my expectation is that Marcus exaggerated the danger. I'm confident he can handle his business, and I'm willing to help, though I hope I don't have to."

"There's no fear? No dread?"

I took a quick survey of the processes between my ears and inside my chest.

"I don't think so," I said.

"One of your good friend's life has been threatened."

"Walking out the door every morning is a risk. If the risk heightens, we handle it," I said.

She fell quiet, but we weren't done. Her muscles were tense and her jaw was set forward. I laced my hands across my stomach and waited.

Ronnie looked youngest without her makeup—the mascara and concealer and the other expensive creams and powders she put on her face made her look more mature, more flawless. But without, her skin was fresh. Her eyelashes natural and unburdened. Without she was less ready for a photoshoot, true, but closer to innocence, to being a girl, a girl who hadn't lived through the uglier side of life. A girl who'd been forced to grow-up far earlier than she should've, a girl who had her innocence stolen through death and sin.

She said, "Earlier I asked Marcus about his marriage. You're correct—the divorce case with Charlotte has me thinking about the nature of happiness and marriage, and my part in it. I'm not struggling with it, but I'm working through it. What are you working through?"

I didn't answer. But I did squint my eyes to let her know I'd heard.

"I'm usually the one who will share what's happening inside, Mackenzie. The good and the bad. And when I ask, you comment that you try not to think about things. But you do. You're human," she said. "The things you think about, or struggle with, or work through, they don't have to pertain to our relationship. But if they do, I'm desperate to hear them. Can I know part of it?"

"Yes."

"Yes what?"

"Yes you can know what's happening inside," I said.

"Good." She smiled. "Tell me."

"I can't."

"Why not?"

"I'm not ready," I said.

"I promise I'll hear your heart like a big girl. That I won't overreact or try to change you. No. That's not true. I promise I'll *try* not to."

"I'm still not ready," I said.

"But you said I can know. I'm right here, listening. Without judgment or moralizing."

"I didn't say you're not ready. I said I'm not ready," I said.

"Mackenzie. That's silly."

"You said without judgment," I said. "You judged me."

"I did. You're right. I perjured myself. I'll rephrase. Mackenzie, what must happen for you to be ready to share with me?"

"Ask me again tomorrow."

"Not tonight."

"No, not tonight."

"You're angry," she said.

"I'm not angry. I'm feeling..." My hands were still laced and I drummed my fingertips, resisting the urge to walk out the bedroom door. "I'm feeling ambushed and defensive."

"Well, I'm feeling lonely and slightly... neglected."

"I always listen to you," I said. "Without judgment or moralizing."

"Relationships are a two-way street. I want to listen. I need to."

"Ask me again tomorrow."

"Why not tonight?" she said.

"Because, Ron, dammit, I told you, I'm not ready."

She threw up her hands and turned away and laid down. "I don't get it."

"You don't have to."

"I love you. I respect you. But I don't understand," she said.

"Ask me again tomorrow."

She made a noncommittal noise and I knew she felt rejected. She'd asked for something and I'd said no. Or I'd said later. And that sucks to hear.

I put my hand on her back and she leaned against it, and we were both angry and solipsistic, but we loved the other, and we fell asleep wounded but together.

In the morning, I felt her rise before dawn and dress and go downstairs. The aroma of coffee drew me up an hour later and I found a note on the kitchen counter.

*Mackenzie,*

*I'm representing a client in DC Federal immigration hearing. I'll return this evening.*

*I apologize for pressuring you last night. That's no way to encourage one's husband to open up. I was worried for Marcus, for us, and wanted to be closer to you. Instead I drove you away.*

*I'll listen to you forever.*
*When you're ready.*
*I love you. But perhaps more importantly, I really like you.*
*-your wife*

I poured some coffee and read it again and I wrote her a note with a pen and I took a picture of it and texted it to her. She texted me back some heart emojis.

Heart emojis.

I searched for a manly and affectionate emoji to respond with but couldn't find anything. If Humphrey Bogart knew what I was doing he would slap me, and tell me only a sissy would be searching for such a thing, a thing that didn't and shouldn't exist.

And that was the whole problem, wasn't it.

## 19

Georgina Princess and I spent the morning in my office doing deep work. Phone off. Computer off. Brain on. Thinking. And pacing. And going outside to pee.

On my desk were two glossy photographs. One of Ervin Lane, and the other Caleb James.

Ervin Lane—big, strong, shaved head, goatee, tattoos visible in his professional cop photo. Drunk. Mean. Angry with Caleb. Angry with the world. But now? Now a humbled, quiet guy with only one hand, working his small farm and cleaning an elementary school at night to make ends meet, healing inside his peaceful new life, hoping I never found Caleb. Being protected by the might of the justice system.

Caleb James—tall, thin, good hair, UVA grad, financial advisor. Addicted to crystal, and dealing with the crap that came along with it, shot a cop. But now? Now a convict on the run, hiding with a big bag of money, clean from methamphetamine, asking me to leave Ervin alone. Being chased by the might of the justice system.

By all accounts, Ervin had been a major league jackass.

Busted down to patrol after being a detective. Living alone. His girlfriend left him. Drunk. But the Ervin I met was a man doing the work to get clean. He was feeding chickens and attending AA meetings and asking me to forgive his attacker. He was struggling to be whole. Well, save for that hard prosthetic hand. Whole except for that.

By all accounts, Caleb was a good guy. He'd been giving out financial advice to the inmates. His father adored him. He'd made such a strong impression on the librarian that he'd been smuggled out, to freedom.

To Mexico?

Maybe. Somehow, I doubted it.

I didn't know why I doubted it, though. The gears of my subconscious were churning and sifting through conversations and facts and churning out inferences and opinions, from whence I knew not. I thought he was close. I thought I was close. Hot on his trail, though I'd made little discernible progress. Maybe he was in Mexico, but maybe, if I ever found him, I'd look back on my investigation and wonder how I didn't see the connections sooner.

We went outside to pee again—the dog, not me—walked to Our Daily Bread for a steak & cheese and coffee. The owner loved GPA and asked if she could please set down a plate of roast beef for her and GPA threatened heartbreak if I didn't acquiesce, so I did, and everyone was happy with everything. We walked back to my office, which was baking in the July heat but damp from the A/C, and I ate my sandwich and drank my coffee, and I picked up my office phone and called Lynchburg. Specifically, I called the prosecutor who handled Caleb James' case, Terrance Goodwin.

His secretary told me I could leave a message, but I declared I had information about Caleb James, and she replied, "One moment, please," and exactly one moment later Terrance Goodwin came on the line. When he realized it was me, his enthusiasm dimmed a couple lumens.

"Mr. August," said Terrance, "I'll listen to whatever you got to say, but I have nothing to add from the last time we spoke. Matter fact, even less."

"You were told not to help me."

"Maybe I was."

"Who told you that?"

"The powers that be."

"Because the powers that be are heavily invested in covering up Ervin's sins. And by extension, their own," I said.

"No comment, my man."

He was lying—I don't think I was his man.

I wondered if he was wearing his brown Air Force One sneakers.

"I have what we clever investigators call a plan."

"Tell me your plan," said Terrance.

"We convince Caleb to turn himself in."

He made a small laughing noise.

"Sounds simple. Let me know when you got him."

"I want to offer Caleb a better deal," I said.

"A better deal?"

"Less jail time. On the condition he returns to prison volitionally."

"Less jail time?" Terrance was repeating stuff, which was my go-to move. "Caleb killed a cop and got off with second degree. Man already got the best deal in history. We don't negotiate with fugitives, August."

"Based on my findings, I believe you should."

"What findings?" said Terrance.

"That Ervin was drunk as a skunk that night. And that

you and everyone else swept that under the rug."

Terrance fell silent. Was I prone to hyperbole, I'd say he fell deathly silent. His career was being threatened. If it came out he'd covered for a cop inebriated on the job, he'd be disbarred. And criminally prosecuted. And here I was, blabbing about it. Most likely he'd inform someone about my threat, maybe the judge, maybe the chief, and we'd either negotiate or I'd be in hot water. But what's the point of being tall and big and intrepid if you couldn't threaten prosecutors? I'd been in hot water before.

"Nobody wants to drag this whole thing into the light," I said. "Not Ervin, not you, not me. I say, we cut Caleb a better deal, one more in line with the fact that the arresting officer was inebriated, and it's over."

"August, even if what you say is true—and it isn't—you have no proof. To be honest, I'm hurt. And offended. You're making a big damn accusation for a man with no proof."

"How about you show me the dashcam from the arrest," I said.

"Sure," he said.

I waited. Because like hell would Terrance show me the dashcam video.

"Sure, as soon as you get a warrant. And good luck with that. Judge Ward will bite your ass off and issue a restraining order," he said. "Or worse."

"Oh dear. Oh dear oh dear," I said.

"You think you're funny—"

"*Wrong*, I know I'm funny."

"—but let me know when you petition the judge. I want to watch the massacre."

"C'mon, let's cut a deal with Caleb. That way you don't have to wrangle with Ronnie Summers," I said.

"Ronnie Summers? Caleb already has an attorney,

Elaine Terry."

"He's about to get an upgrade."

I could almost hear Terrance chewing on his lip.

"You have Ronnie Summers on retainer?" he said.

"Even better. I'm sleeping with her."

He laughed. And it hurt my pride.

"Yeah. Sure you are. I've met Ronnie Summers, my man. Girl's out of your league."

"First, you're right. Second, ouch. Third, I got bad news for you," I said.

"What's that?"

"Check the court documents. Ronnie's married. To one stalwart, fearless, and hilarious private investigator Mackenzie August."

"Bull shit."

"Which part? Some of that could be debatable, but not the hilarious part."

"You're married to Veronica Summers," said Terrance.

"I am."

"Bull shit."

"Even worse for you, she's the one who proposed," I said.

Which was true.

Mostly true.

He made a big inhale. "I don't buy it. But. Let's say I did..." He paused to reassess. Regroup. Rethink. And rejoin. He let all the air out, and said *Damn* under his breath. "Even if Counselor Summers represents Caleb, that changes nothing. There's no evidence Ervin was drunk. And we don't negotiate with fugitives so they'll return to prison. That's absurd."

"Let me see the video," I said.

"No. Hey. August. Be real. You're hitched to *the* Ronnie Summers?"

"Goodbye, Terrance. You'll be hearing from Caleb's attorney soon."

I ended the call and set the phone down.

GPA stood and her head cocked to the side in expectation.

*Oh boy you are bluffing, yes, I know that you are, that was a bluff, but we should go for a walk maybe and I will love you anyway if we don't but maybe we should.*

"It's not a bluff," I told her. "Or, it's only seventy-five percent of a bluff."

I hadn't mentioned any of this to Ron. But I could, and that made me dangerous.

I told GPA to be patient, that I needed to make another phone call. She laid down again, broken-hearted but full of fidelity.

Robin Lucas, according to the Lynchburg grapevine, had been dating Ervin Lane before dumping him and 'homie-hopping' to Caleb James. Soon after his arrest, she'd moved.

I had questions.

Had Robin in fact homie-hopped?

Had she moved because she was pregnant?

Where was she now?

Had she seen Caleb since his escape?

Would she consider shackling him and driving him to me?

I need an inroad with her.

I researched Robin online. She either had no social media or, more likely, she maintained accounts under a pseudonym. Neither Caleb nor Ervin had Facebook or Instagram, that I knew of, so I couldn't research backwards in their timelines for Robin. Instead I focused on her parents. I googled Lynchburg Lucas Family and got a dozen leads and wrote them on a legal pad. Running those names into Facebook quickly eliminated half. I used Facebook because Robin's parents would be of the age where it was still relevant, instead of, say, Tinder or TikTok. Which were websites of sorcery and witchcraft.

After an hour of investigating with fingers that made my laptop look small, I zeroed in on Maggie Lucas. She was a nice-looking woman in her fifties, maybe late fifties, who lived in Lynchburg and liked to post photos of her family, which included a young woman about Robin's age. I walked backwards in time on her account, scanning photos, until I found a shot taken at a beach, three years ago, and Maggie listed her family by name, including her daughter Robin.

Boom. Pow. Bang.

Mackenzie August, cyber stalker extraordinaire.

Robin Lucas was a looker, if you were into tall thin willowy brunettes. Her facial architecture was strong— pointy chin, prominent cheekbones—but more like an athletic scientist than a girl with an eating disorder. A hiker! That's what she was, look at those calves. She looked like the kinda person who stayed in Lynchburg because she liked the mountains, and she walked them in worn-out Columbia boots and a backpack, and got second glances from the hikers she passed.

I called Samantha Miller, queen of Lynchburg, knower and purveyor of people, but she didn't answer. I texted her instead of leaving a message.

**— Mrs. Miller, I need the cell number of Robin Lucas, daughter of Maggie Lucas. Pretty please. Use your connections and Baptist resources.**

She didn't answer immediately and I'd already been in my office for hours and hours, staring at a tiny computer screen, and GPA was whining, so I made like Caleb James and got the hell out of there.

## 20

That night Kix and I read books in my bed until he fell asleep. He liked the Berenstain Bears. Maybe he didn't know exactly what was going on, but he laughed when Papa Bear fell down and got injured. I tried not to take that personally.

He was sleeping against the pillow beside me, mouth slightly agape like a cherub, when Ronnie arrived and chimes played in my ears.

She did a little gasp. "He's so beautiful it hurts. I swear, Mackenzie, my heart actually fucking hurts."

"We have that in common."

"Sorry for saying fuck," she said. "God, I don't want him to ever age."

"He never will. Heroes don't."

"But he has. He's bigger than he used to be, maybe since this morning." Ronnie stepped out of her shoes and removed her belt, and perched on the edge of our bed and yawned and said, "I'm hungry but I'm more tired than hungry. It was a long day."

"Did you win?"

"Mackenzie. Of course I won."

"Want me to cook something?" I said.

"No thank you. I want you to lay next to me as I fall asleep."

She stepped into the closet to change and I carried Kix to his room, where GPA had already posted herself as a sentry. When I came out, Ronnie was in the bathroom, beginning her facial cleansing routine. Nine hours later she finished as I was about to drift off.

She slid into bed and she brought with her an aroma of perfume, expensive creams, astringent cleansers, and minty toothpaste.

"It was not nine hours," she said.

"Feels like it."

"Are you ready?"

"For sex. Always."

"I'm too tired to please my husband. I'll make it up to you tomorrow, maybe twice. What I mean is, are you ready to tell me what you're feeling? Last night you weren't. If you still aren't, I understand. No pressure."

"If you're too tired to please your husband, then your husband could be the—"

"Mackenzie. Focus on my words. Not my boobs."

"Impossible," I said.

Under the covers she kicked me.

"About last night," I said. "And my emotions. I've been dwelling on them."

"Yes."

"You caught me off guard and I reacted defensively. Your request was understandable, even healthy, and I apologize."

"All records have been wiped clean. Proceed."

"You want me to share what I feel. About you, about us, about the world. Something intimate. Something you don't know. Something that will let you get closer, to show I trust you."

"If you're trying to arouse me, it's working," she said.

"Okay. Here goes." I had reading glasses folded over the collar of my shirt, but I slid them off and set them onto my nightstand and I pulled the string on my lamp. The room darkened and I slid farther down, so my head was on the pillow. The absurdly expensive pillow. "Emotions are hard for me."

"Why?"

"Shh."

"Sorry Mackenzie. Go on."

"Emotions are hard for me to share. For two reasons, I think. The first is simple—I often don't know what I feel. Last night you asked if I was worried about Marcus. I didn't know. Because the information was new and I was still processing it and the emotions weren't important," I said.

"Not important?"

"Marcus said his life is in danger. That set off a flurry of inner mechanisms for me, mostly around keeping you safe, keeping Kix safe, the implications for me, for Manny, for Roanoke, for Marcus himself. How I felt about his danger was irrelevant. If a man pulls a gun on me, I can't stop and process my emotions. I act. That's the way my whole life is. I walk through my day and I act, and looking back on it later I might identify some of the emotions involved, but only at a distance. Asking me what I feel in a moment will be frustrating and fruitless for you, because I don't know. But, I could probably tell you how I felt about something that happened two days ago."

I was on my back, looking upward into the dark. She was on her side, looking at me.

"Do you think that's a personality defect?" she said.

"No. It's just me. Here's what I mean. You're hyper competitive. You judge yourself against other women, against other attorneys, you brag about victories, you're hard on yourself when you don't annihilate the opposition. One of the first things you told me about yourself is that you were worried one of the girls in your apartment building had better hamstrings than you. She had been a gymnast, so you were doubling-up on your exercises. Is that a personality defect?"

I couldn't see that she was smiling but I could hear it. "I'm feeling attacked."

"You shouldn't. It's not a defect. It's a trait of your personality."

"For the record, mine were better than hers," she said.

"You see? Do you hear yourself?"

"Yes. I do. But facts are facts."

"It's not a defect. Nor is my emotional dissonance. It simply takes me longer than you."

"Manny always knows what he feels. He talks about his emotions a lot," she said.

"Manny is a sissy. And if you leave me for him, so you can have quicker access to emotions, you'll be fighting over night cream and bathroom time. It'll be untenable."

She yawned and filled the space between us with mint. Ronnie maintained exceptionally clean teeth. She nightly brushed her tongue and gums. She said, "I don't want another man's emotions, Mackenzie. I want yours. Even if it takes longer. What's the other thing? You said there were two. This is fun, by the way."

"The other reason emotions are hard is because it's the most private thing about me. The most private, ergo the most precious, the most valuable. Also the most embarrassing, the most intimate. Which means I don't share them. I don't expose myself. I don't let myself be vulnerable. In other words, I don't trust you with them."

"Hey," she said.

"And that is a personality defect, I think. Because you've proven to be trustworthy. Ergo I should trust you. And I'll work on it."

She had closed her eyes, I knew, because the hallway ambience was no longer reflecting back at me from her side. "And I promise to always be respectful of them. Your emotions, I mean. Or, I promise to always try."

"Thank you."

"But Mackenzie, listen, I'm so so tired. Please stop talking about how you feel."

I laughed and she moved her face against my shoulder and I felt her smile.

"If I could have sex with any man on earth right now, it would be you. But I think I'm too tired," she said.

"Who would be second, of any man on earth?"

"Burt Reynolds."

"He's dead," I said.

"Sean Connery."

"Also dead."

"Marlon Brando," she said.

"The hell's wrong with you?"

"Jim Morrison."

"Never mind. Forget I asked," I said.

"Young Elvis."

"Ahhh. You finally got one right."

## 21

I was driving into Lynchburg when Mrs. Samantha Miller returned my call.

"Mr. August, you asked about Robin Lucas? Have I got a tale to tell you." She said it with enough enthusiasm that I pulled over. The morning sun was high and hot and I kept the motor running for the air conditioning.

"I'm all ears."

"Betty Simpkins is friends with Maggie Lucas, so I called her, of course, but Betty had a falling out with Maggie's mother over something-or-other, I forget what, but Betty put me on to Janis Burns. Janis knows the whole story, top to bottom, and she gave me everything, every rose and thorn. Want to hear it?"

"More than anything."

"Well. Maggie Lucas always loved Caleb James, since he was a teenager. Can you imagine her mortification now? How awful. Caleb and her daughter Robin, the girl you called about, they used to be sweethearts in high school and stayed together when he left for UVA. Halfway through their sophomore year, they broke up. She attended

Randolph, of course. Janis thinks Caleb was unfaithful, and I'm inclined to agree based on what we know now, but there's no proof. No hard proof, is that what you'd say? Anyway. They both graduated and Caleb moved north for a hoity-toity internship and Robin, bless her heart, takes up with a local police officer named Ervin Lane. Can you believe that?"

I could. I already knew it. But I let her have the victory.

"Oh my," I said.

"I *know*. I like to fell over. The juiciest gossip I've ever heard. How did we not know? I feel sorry for the man, but he didn't deserve Robin Lucas, gorgeous creature. *Anyway*. Eventually Caleb James returned from New York to open his private financial firm, and Janis was hazy on the *hard facts* here, as Maggie either didn't know or didn't want to share, but it sounds like Robin Lucas rekindled her romance with Caleb while *still* dating Ervin. She may be gorgeous, but she should know nothing good comes from dating two men. That's in the Bible."

"Is it?" I said.

"Somewhere, I'm certain."

"Where's Robin now?"

"The story is not complete, Mr. August. Be patient," she said.

"Sorry."

"Robin was openly dating Ervin. But she was with Caleb *on the side*. Now, Janis doesn't know the exact order of events, but here's what she thinks—Caleb proposed to her, she said yes but they kept it secret, she broke up with Ervin, but then Robin discovered Caleb's drug habit and called things off, and soon after Ervin pulled Caleb over and Caleb tries to murder him. Lord have mercy. Have all the mercy."

"Was Robin pregnant?"

"Janis never mentioned it. Why? What have you heard?" she said.

"I know nothing. Only curious. Where is Robin now?"

"She moved! I forgot that part. Maybe out of embarrassment. Her sin found her out. She took a job teaching in Halifax."

"Halifax. Can anything good come out of Halifax?" I said.

A short silence. "I suppose. I always thought it a lovely place."

"I was quoting the Bible. You'll have to take my word for it."

"Will the love triangle will help you catch Caleb?"

"It might. Do you have her phone number?"

"In fact," said Samantha, "I do! You're not the only detective, are you."

"Scary thought."

STILL IN MY CAR, parked on the side of 460 and being buffeted by large trucks, I discovered Robin Lucas' number was disconnected. I tried her three times, and got the Not In Service message each. Thanks a lot, Samantha the detective.

I called Halifax Public School's H.R. department, and Ms. Myers answered.

I said, "Hi Ms. Myers, this is Bob Fitzgerald at the high school? How are you this beautiful morning? I'm trying to get ahold of Robin Lucas and I believe I must have an outdated number."

"Robin Lucas?" I listened to keys clicking. "Robin Lucas left last year."

"Rats. Double rats. She left some belongings in my room

I just discovered. Can I give you her phone number and you tell me if I have it right?" I read the number out loud and Ms. Myers said, "You have it correct... What did you say your name was?"

"Sorry, Ms. Myers, it's Bob. At the high school. Remind me, did Robin teach at Clay Mills Elementary?"

"No, sir, it was Cluster Springs."

"Thanks, Ms. Myers, I'll give them a call."

And I did. The secretary at Cluster Springs announced herself as Lori Lawrence and I said, "Hi Lori, it's Bob Fitzgerald over at central office. Listen, I'm working with Human Resources to find Robin Lucas. Believe it or not, we only realized her bank account closed before her final paycheck went through. That money's just been a'sitting there for months. I called her but her line's been disconnected. So has her school email account, obviously. You don't have any way to reach Ms. Lucas, do you?"

"Hold on, now. Let me check. Ahh, here we go. No, I don't have an alternate phone number. You say she never got her final paycheck?" said Lori Lawrence, the secretary at Cluster Springs.

"Isn't that wild? Ms. Myers about had a heart attack," I said.

"Well, she'd be doing us all a favor, wouldn't she," said Lori Lawrence and I laughed and laughed.

"Listen, who might have a second phone number or email for Robin? I need to forward a check."

"You might try Alethia Ramsay? She and Robin were thick," said Lori Lawrence

"Alethia Ramsay." I wrote it down on a note pad in the passenger seat. "Do you happen to have a number for Ms. Ramsay? So's I don't need to bother Ms. Myers again, God save me."

Lori Lawrence laughed and gave me the phone number and I called Alethia Ramsay, whoever that was, and Alethia answered and I gave her my spiel—human resources trying to get ahold of Robin Lucas about her closed bank account.

Alethia said she hadn't heard from Robin. Robin vanished after leaving Halifax and Alethia had no good working number for her. But wait, hang on, she had an email. They'd exchanged personal emails a handful of times over a disaster of a game night attempted that winter. Wait one second, she'd find it, she'd just do a search on her phone while I waited on speaker phone, any second now, when had that been... ah hah! Here it was, ready? Alethia read the email address and I wrote it down on the pad and thanked her.

Well.

I looked at the email address. With distaste and reluctance. It was hard to surprise and pressure someone over email.

But beggars can't be choosers, or some trite platitude to make myself feel better.

I wrote Robin.

**Ms. Lucas,**

**My name's Mackenzie August and I'm a private detective. I've learned a lot about Ervin and Caleb and you, and we need to talk. It's everyone versus Caleb right now. Everyone except for me. I'm his best hope. A phone call hurts nobody.**

**-Mackenzie**

And I listed my phone number.

It was a garbage email message and I hated it as soon as I sent it.

CALEB HAD PICKED up a cocaine habit in New York City, so the story ran. Returning to Lynchburg, with less money and less access to coke, he switched to meth. According to the police chief, his dealer had been a man named Marky. I'd banged on Marky's door last week and it was time to do so again.

He lived in a trailer in Timberlake off Stable. It wasn't set in a trailer park, or if it was each trailer had a huge lot with scrubby trees hiding the neighbors. Marky's trailer had a gravel drive that needed replenishment, and overgrown weeds, and an old truck, and the strong scent of dog feces.

I banged on the door, which was flimsy and wanted to break, and a dog inside yowled at me. I banged some more and tried calling to Marky but I could barely hear myself over the barking, so I squatted on my haunches and sweet-talked the dog in a high pitched voice. I used all the good words *way up high*. The door was ajar enough that we could see one another through a gap, and soon the dog wasn't angry but so so so excited to be friends. The dog was whining and I was cooing, "*Hi! Hi there! Who's a good girl!*" and the animal was trying to lick my fingers.

A man's voice said, "Got'damn it, Outlaw, you ain't good for shit, are you," and I felt footsteps. I remained in a squat but I scooted backward. The door opened and Outlaw rushed out. He was a long-haired breed that I couldn't identify, and we were already fast friends.

Marky wore flipflops and jeans that were too large and had a dozen little singed holes in the thighs where he'd burned them with cigarettes when bored. He was shirtless and too thin and dragons were tattooed up both sides of his ribs, the tails curling to his shoulders.

A fetid stench rolled out and it turned my stomach.

"Better show me a warrant, jackass." In Marky's mouth

was an extinguished cigarette butt. His hair looked like he wanted to keep it buzzed but got tired of doing it three weeks ago.

"Good morning to you too, Marky."

"Warrant." He snapped his fingers.

His face was pock marked. Meth mites was the name given to the facial scarring of crystal methamphetamine addicts, but the scars didn't come from real bugs—they came because the addict imagined he felt bugs under his skin and so he scratched at them. A lot. He scratched until he bled and took chunks out of his face and then he did it again the next night. Tearing at bugs that didn't exist.

Don't do drugs, kids.

"Marky, I'm not a cop. I'm looking for Caleb James."

"Caleb James." He snorted and accidentally jettisoned the cigarette butt. "And you think my ass is keeping him here?"

"I can't imagine a better place."

"Any place is better than this place," he said.

"I have some questions for you and then I'll leave."

"I don't know where Caleb's at and I hope you don't find 'im," said Marky.

"He came to see you after he busted out. It was the first place he visited."

"I already tole the police that." Marky absently patted his jean pockets. Maybe for more cigarettes.

"He needed another hit?"

"Yeah. Yeah sure." Marky turned his attention to the rotted wooden porch I squatted on, looking for half-used cigarettes. He kicked at his dog and said, "Move, Outlaw, dammit."

"That's what you told the police."

"Right. We done? I was watching... something."

"Then where'd he go?" I said.

"What?"

"Caleb James. He left here and went where?"

"Got no idea."

"He came here for meth," I said.

"Yep. You already asked that."

"Here's the thing. I don't believe you."

"You got any smokes on you?" he said.

"Answer my questions and I'll give you five bucks for another pack. And I said I don't believe you."

He screwed up one eye like the sun hurt and looked at me, maybe for the first time. "Don't believe me?"

"No."

"Well. I guess. I don't give one dog shit if you believe me or not."

"Caleb was clean. The police assume he came here to get crystal, but I don't believe it. He was clean and busting out of prison for a reason, and that reason wasn't to return to his addictions. I want his real impetus for coming here," I said.

"His what? We ain't gay."

"Marky. Read a book."

"You ain't a cop?"

"No I am not."

"You gotta tell me if you are," said Marky. "I know my rights."

"That's not one of your rights. I'm a private cop. I have no power to arrest you. Here's the deal, Marky. I think Caleb got screwed. I'm trying to help him," I said. It was kinda true. "Anything you tell me, helps him."

"I used to deal. I don't anymore."

"Caleb didn't come here for a hit, did he." I was scratching Outlaw behind his big ugly ears and he would never move as long as it continued. He was panting and smiling and looking everywhere.

"What's a private cop?"

"I hire out to people. Do hard things they don't want to do. Ever watch, ah, Magnum P.I.?"

"Yeah, I seen those reruns. Guy with a mustache." He was patting his pants pockets again.

"That's me. Caleb didn't come here for a hit, did he."

"Guy with the mustache drives a nice car," said Marky.

"You didn't give Caleb any crystal."

"No. No sir I did not. That's what I tole the cops. I tole them I don't deal no more."

"I don't believe that part, but let's move on. What'd he want?" I said.

"He wanted..." Marky turned to look inside his home. Any cigarettes inside he forgot about?

"Focus, Marky. I'll buy you a whole carton. Why'd Caleb come here?"

He grinned then. "Oh yeah. I remember. A whole carton? I remember. Caleb wanted me to get clean."

"He came here to tell you that?"

"Yeah. Go to rehab, Marky, he said."

"That's it? Why didn't he call you?" I asked.

"Ahhh..."

"What else did he say? Or do?"

"Caleb? Caleb gave me the name and the telephone number of a rehab place. Said he'd pay for a week, if I went."

"Which one?"

"How do I know? I asked for the money and he said he'd pay the place directly. Tricky sum'bitch, ain't he."

"Which rehab place?" I said.

"I forget. Threw the paper away."

"Was he going there?"

"Going where?"

"Was Caleb going to the rehab place?" I said.

"He was fucking clean! Why would he go there?"

"Great question. Where did he go?"

"Took off up the road, I expect," said Marky.

"Heading where?"

"I don't know."

"Mexico?" I said.

"Yeah! Mexico, man. He mentioned Mexico."

"Was anyone with him?"

"I didn't ask. He only stayed a minute."

"What kinda car?" I said.

"He woke me up. I was in bed. Shit, that's right." Marky kinda laughed. "I was with Meredith then. He woke me up and Meredith was there, her tits hanging out. I never saw his car. Shit." He laughed more about Meredith.

"On his way to Mexico."

"Yep. He made some dumbass joke about looking him up if I was ever there. Like I want to go to the place that makes all the Mexicans. I wonder where Meredith ran off to?"

"Has he called you since?"

"No he ain't called me. No no no, wait. No, wait, yeah he did. Yeah he did once. Meredith was gone by then, pretty sure," he said.

"Where was he?"

"Tole you, got no idea. Mexico I assume."

"How long ago?"

"Dunno, a few months. It was colder."

"What'd he say?"

He made a grunt. "Huh?"

"When Caleb called you, what'd he say, Marky?"

"Said I should go to rehab. Some place in Kentucky or Tennessee. Maybe West Virginia? Hell, I don't know," he said.

"What number did he call from?"

"That was two or three phones ago, man, don't ask me to look it up cause I can't."

Outlaw whined, looking over my shoulder.

I heard the arrival of an engine. Tires crunching gravel. The sudden whoop of a police siren and the trailer walls turned blue. Lynchburg police.

"Oh got'damn it, you said you weren't cops."

"Bet you five bucks, Marky," I said, "they're here for me. Not you."

## 22

Patrolman Jonas Whiteside was thick in the chest and fore-arms and had a great chin. Could play a decent superhero in a kid's movie. He said, "Chief wants to see you," and I said, "Sure," and standing by his car I asked him if he'd been tight with Ervin Lane. He didn't respond. I asked if Ervin had once been a detective but got busted down for alcohol? Whiteside said, "Stop being a dumb shit and follow my car," and he got back in his cruiser and made a U-turn and I got into mine and did the same, and Marky was fingering a twenty-dollar bill and thinking about cigarettes.

We caravanned downtown to Court Street and braked at the police department. Whiteside walked me past the front desk, still manned by the same cop who was too fat to do anything else, and to Police Chief Jake Robertson's office. The office was hotter than it'd been last time, and the chief was still as short and fiery.

He wore his dress blues, possibly for my benefit, with four stars on his shoulder. A lot easier to become a chief of police in a small city like Lynchburg than it was in Los

Angeles, where maybe he'd be a lieutenant by now. Not that he was bad at his job, but there was less competition.

He jabbed a thick finger at me.

"I suppose if you're gonna keep running around and trying to do my job, I could at least show you something that might help, August. I told you to knock this shit off, but you didn't, and here we are. I'd like to throw you in jail a couple days but I don't see how I could manage it, so instead have a look at this."

"Good morning," I said.

On his desk sat a laptop and he used a finger to swivel it around. He mashed the space bar and the video began. It was a police dashcam, kinda distorted and jumpy the way they always seemed to be. I sat in the chair opposite him to see better. A white BMW 3 was parked on the side of the road, seen from the point of view of the police cruiser's windshield. The BMW was flashing shades of blue, reflecting the emergency lights. Behind the car I could see it was night. Ervin Lane walked toward the BMW and my gut clinched—I was about to witness him lose a hand and Kim Harper be shot to death.

Ervin stopped at the open window of the BMW and spoke with the driver. There was no sound, because either Kim wasn't making any or she was out of the car. In the glare of the cruiser's headlights I looked for and found the tattoos on Ervin's forearms and the back of his neck. At least thirty pounds heavier than when I'd met him in Indiana.

I asked, "No body cameras?"

"No body cameras," said the chief. "And no external audio."

Was Ervin drunk in the video? I couldn't tell. He walked steadily enough. He stood another minute at the window, shifting his weight, shining a flashlight through the front and rear window. Talking about what? Robin?

Ervin stepped backwards and started shouting. Then Kim Harper strode uncertainly into the picture. She'd been standing off to the right of the BMW, out of sight. She took a position at the rear passenger door, opposite Ervin, one hand on her belt, the other holding the radio receiver on her shoulder.

The driver door opened and Caleb James stood out of the car. He looked pale and sweaty and emaciated. He was shouting and Ervin was too, and I could hear their muffled voices but I'd need a few more listens to discern any words.

Caleb was screaming. *Screaming* screaming. He'd admitted he'd been high as a kite and he looked it.

He either lunged at Ervin or stumbled. No matter, they made contact.

Ervin fumbled at something on his belt—couldn't get it. Harper looked confused—she started walking around the front of the BMW. She spoke into the receiver on her shoulder and her voice came through the radio inside the car—*Squad eighteen. Driver resisting arrest. Request backup.*

The powerful transmission from dispatch came next —*Copy squad eighteen, driver resisting arrest. Squad nine, 10-33 on Hollins Mill.*

Another voice, male—*Copy 10-33 on Hollins Mill. Squad nine en route.*

*Copy squad nine en route.*

"He's trying to get his pepper spray," said Chief Robertson, and I was startled out of my viewing. "All our officers carry them. Trained to go for their spray instead of their firearm."

But Ervin couldn't get it. His fingers wouldn't cooperate.

Then the men were hitting each other. No contest—

Ervin was a giant in comparison, and he had Caleb by the neck, pushing him down, Caleb punching at Ervin's stomach. Here, Ervin looked drunk—looked like a man coordinating his movements from far away. Slow, dizzy, man. Caleb slipped free and turned to run, Ervin grabbed him by the back of his shirt. He had Caleb's shirt in his left hand, and his right was still scrabbling at his belt, Caleb still screaming in his hysteria, words now audible.

*Let go, let go, Ervin, let me GOOOO.*

The men spilled off screen.

On screen, the BMW reflected blue lights and Kim Harper was shouting, coming around the car, one hand on her shoulder, the other holding pepper spray, looked like.

—*Squad eighteen, driver engaged with Officer Lane! 10-33, I need backup.*

—*Copy squad eighteen, Officer Lane engaged. All cars, 10-33 on Hollins Mill.*

"Now listen to this," said the chief.

Kim Harper walking left on the screen, her face canted toward her shoulder, toward the radio.

BOOM.

A gunshot.

"There. You heard. Sumbitch Caleb has Ervin's gun and shot him. Blows through his wrist," said the chief.

How'd he get Ervin's gun?

Harper wasn't moving. Watching, not speaking into her radio...

"And..." said the chief.

BOOM.

Another gun shot.

Kim Harper was hit. In the throat. It wasn't immediately a mess but the impact was obvious. She grabbed at it, stumbling backward. Both hands at her neck. She fell into the glare of the BMW's headlights, and the chief reached over the laptop and smacked the spacebar again and the scene froze.

Harper was visible from the shoulders down, her face hidden behind a tire. Paused mid squirm and I felt sick.

"Awful," I said.

"That woman died making a traffic stop and here you are, flying to Indiana to harass the other officer who got shot. That woman died and you're calling up my prosecutor, asking to cut a deal else you'll tell the world the arresting officer who got maimed was drunk and should be held accountable, instead of the man who actually pulled the trigger!" He was roaring now and it was hard on my ears. "That woman died and you're grilling my deputy about if Ervin had been a detective but got busted down because of alcohol, like you're trying to pin this God-awful thing on him!"

"Ervin admitted he was drunk that night. If we cut Caleb a better deal—"

"I don't give one got'damn about cutting him a deal! There will be no deals." Sweat poured down the chief's bald head. He swiveled the laptop around, smashing keys and the track pad with violence, and then faced it toward me. "Hit the space bar, August."

I did.

Another video, this time security from inside a jail, high up on a wall looking down. A grayish hallway. Two men walking away from the camera, looked like prison guards. This video was of higher resolution and clarity. Then chaos. Silent chaos. A lunatic leaped into the screen from an adjoining hallway and launched himself on the two men. A lunatic in an orange jumpsuit. One of the men fell and the lunatic in the jumpsuit started hitting and kicking him and the second man tried to pull him off.

"That's Caleb, the man you're defending. He attacked the guards and tried to make a getaway. Always trying to escape, isn't he, the piece of shit. The prison guard, Walters, needed twelve stitches."

The screen went dark, the video ended.

Me and Robertson and his furnace glare.

"I don't understand why you claim to be chasing a fugitive but all I hear are got'damn stories about you trying to pin this thing on Ervin, a man who's trying to get his life together after being disabled. I don't understand it one bit, August. No no no, shut up. We're done talking. You don't get to speak. You go on and get the hell out, and remember who the good guy is, August, and who's the bad guy."

"That's the thing, Chief." I stood. "I'm not sure we have those here."

He pointed with a stubby thick finger at the door and I left his office. His anger had mine triggered in response, and I knew I should leave before emotions rose higher.

I felt sick watching Kim Harper be shot. The real victim in this mess that somehow was forgotten.

Not much in the videos was good for my idea of cutting a deal. If Ervin had done anything wrong that night, it wasn't egregious. Or if it was, it was off screen. It'd be hard to prove he was drunk unless he confessed under oath, while Caleb appeared insane. Watching those clips, I couldn't blame the cops for being furious with me.

Something about the arrest video bothered me, though. Maybe it was that Chief Robertson hadn't shown me the whole clip. Both videos had been cut in such a way that I couldn't see what happened after—

I was walking the police department hallway toward

the front desk, and something hit me in the head. *Crack*. Hard and mean and it came from the dark doorway I passed. Hot pressure, white pain. I stumbled sideways and something else hard and mean hit me from the other side. The impacts knocked logic clean out of my head. Couldn't think clearly to defend. Couldn't recognize I should. Something was bad but I didn't know what. Dizzy, the world not on its axis. Another hit and me too loopy to care.

Me on the ground. On all fours. Maybe. Brain spinning.

I saw a boot before impact. Kicked hard in the face like punting a ball. Busted my nose.

Some survival instinct told me to move, move move. Crawling. Crawling. Noise behind me. Mackenzie August, an undignified mess.

I blinked at the pain behind my eyes. Inside my eyes.

I was in a dark room. Under a table. I'd crawled there. Blood on my face, blood on my hands.

A man in a bright doorway. Two men behind him. Three total.

The man put his hands on his knees, squatting, and peered at me. The men behind laughing.

"Damn, August. What happened. You fell over pretty hard, huh," said the man. Whiteside. Big forearms. In his left hand he gripped a blackjack. "You hit your head on the door or something?"

"Or something," said the guy behind him. All men wearing police uniforms.

"Ouch," I said.

"Yeah, looks like ouch, you big motherfucker."

"Took all three of you," I said. Stupidly. But there wasn't a lot great to say, under a table, the hell beaten out of you.

"While you're down here," said Whiteside. I couldn't see

him well, limned in hallway light, light that hurt my eyes. "Let's have a friendly chat."

I had a concussion.

I was concussed.

And blood on my shirt, one of my favorite shirts from Vineyard Vines, dammit. I told GPA I might be getting in hot water. Never wear your favorite shirts when you're in hot water.

Whiteside was saying, "About our boy Ervin. Ervin Lane. We appreciate that you're gonna leave him alone. That you're gonna quit making bad suggestions about our boy Ervin. You follow what I'm saying?"

"I'm having trouble. Use smaller words."

"Police brutality. How's that for smaller," he said.

"Brutality is four syllables, you idiot. That's not small at all."

"Ervin Lane. You stay away. You get the hell off his case or you'll fall down harder next time."

We were in an interrogation room. The kind with a one-way mirror and cameras. They wouldn't risk jumping me with a camera potentially running. I was safe.

Safe-ish.

And concussed.

And my damn shirt.

"You owe me a shirt," I said.

"I owe you an ass beating, is what I owe you."

"Whiteside, the next time we have a run in, I don't think it's gonna go so well for you."

Hard to sound scary when your mouth wasn't working great, one of your eyes already swelling shut.

"Is that a threat?" He shifted in his squat. "Are you threatening an officer? It sounds that way. Please tell me you are."

"Hey." Guy behind him set a hand on Whiteside's shoulder. "This is taking too long. Let's go."

"You guys go before I get a second wind," I said.

"Keep it up, August."

"C'mon," said the guy. I didn't know him. "Now."

"Yeah yeah." Whiteside stood. Hooked the blackjack on his belt. "Careful on your way out, August. These doorways can sneak up on you."

The three men in uniform left. Fading footsteps and then the distant sound of a door. Gone.

I was alone.

I leaned backward against the leg of the table and took a deep breath. Through my mouth, because my nose was already clotting.

Hiding under a table, like all winsome and fearless detectives.

## 23

Heroes are supposed to win fights, no matter the odds. Jack Reacher never lost, did he? But sometimes the bad guys are behind you and pulverize you with blackjacks before you're ready. The hero could be forgiven for this, but he still felt like an ass, walking to his car with a head full of screws, ready to get the hell out of dodge.

In the mirror my reflection bordered on hilarity. My lip was swelling. My eye purple. My nose bleeding.

Hilarious and heartbreaking.

I should put it to work. There's an idea.

I braked at the end of Court Street.

Might as well. I was low on epiphanies.

I reversed and parallel parked on the street in front of a covey of law offices, the bottom floor belonging to Terry & Graham Law Firm.

I didn't want to do this. I wanted to drive home and chew ibuprofen and stick my head in the freezer. But Jack Reacher would *never*.

Sally Gardner sat contented at her desk. She was both the receptionist and paralegal for Terry and for Graham, and she liked to hold my hand. She wore a flowery dress and she stood and made the appropriate gasp when I walked in.

When I stumbled in.

"Oh my stars," she said.

"Good morning, Sally."

"Mr. August, what happened?"

"Nice to be remembered. I've been running around the state and thought you'd forgotten me." I kinda winced and dabbed at my lip with a tissue from my car.

She came around the desk and took my hand and squeezed it. "You poor thing, what *happened*?"

"I'm working on the Caleb James case. Is Elaine in?"

"Mr. August, you're hurt! Car wreck? I didn't hear anything."

"No my car's fine, thank goodness. Thank *heavens*."

With my clogged nose, sounded like, *Thang hebens*.

"You look like death warmed over. Sit down. Sit down here, there's still blood coming from..." She let go of my hand to take my face and tilt it to the side for a better look. She had to reach up. "There's still blood coming from *everywhere*. Sit. Sit here."

I shrugged off her attention.

I pretended to shrug off her attention.

"I'm okay, Sally. Is Elaine in?"

"*Sit.*"

I sat.

She hurried into the bathroom and returned with a medical kit and a wet washcloth. "I haven't seen a face like that since my boy went tea over kettle on his BMX bike. And no, Ms. Terry isn't in."

"Shucks."

She dabbed at two spots on my head and the washcloth came away crimson. And also it really really hurt. Had I been one inch less a man, I'd have tears in my eyes. Jack Reacher would be sobbing.

I never cared for him much.

"Well, Mr. August." She bent to peer at my nose and lip and eye. Her glasses made her eyes huge. She used the washcloth to scrub away blood on my chin threatening to crust. And it really really hurt. "There's not much to be done for your poor face."

"Other than admire it."

"Nothing looks broken or in need of stitches. It'll take time, sweetie, is all. These things do. I'll put some antiseptic on your scalp, though. The skin's wide open there, wide as a cattle gate."

"I appreciate it."

She dabbed more with the washcloth and took a tube of ointment from her kit.

"Please tell me what happened, Mr. August, so I don't have to ask again."

"I'm looking into the Caleb James case. Some of the locals aren't happy about it."

"Someone beat you up? But you're so *big*," she said and that hurt worst of all. "It must have been ten of them, I guess? Who? We'll call the police."

I made a noise, elegiac and dolorous.

"That won't help, I'm afraid, Sally."

"Oh heavens." She lowered the tube and stepped away. Her expression changed to grave, but not quite dolorous. I bet Reacher didn't even know what it meant. "It was the police. Wasn't it. I know it was, you don't need to answer. It was Jackson and Ben Whiteside. Even Jake Robertson can be a horse's rear-end, pardon the expression."

"They're hiding something," I said, "And they know I

know it." With my clogged nose, sounded like, *An they doh I doh id*.

"Hiding something." She was silent a few heartbeats too long.

I nodded and screwed up one eye and snorted.

"You mean, about Ervin Lane and Caleb James, don't you, Mr. August. About the night poor Kim Harper died," she said.

"It's already ruined three people's lives. I'm worried it'll be more, Sally."

The door behind us opened. Someone walked in and strode up the stairs, old woodwork creaking in a dignified way. They didn't comment on the massacre that was me.

"Mr. August, don't you reckon you should leave it alone, then?"

"I can't, Sally. I can't."

"Good lord, why not? Looks to me like it's cost you plenty."

"Because the truth matters, Sally," I said.

"That's true." She said it slowly. "But…"

"I believe in a world where truth and justice are worth fighting for. Lynchburg is worth fighting for. And the only thing necessary for evil to flourish is for good men to do nothing. Someone is lying and covering things up, Sally. And if I don't do something about it, who will? Someone's got to," I said. "Someone's got to."

It was a rousing speech. And a good one. And it was true, though hackneyed enough that I wanted to stomp my own foot. She probably knew I was being dramatic but also saw the kernel of truth within it.

She faced away and packed her medical kit. Returned to the bathroom and I heard water running. She walked into the kitchen from the bathroom, and came back holding a bottle of water.

"Sweetie, take this. Drink it. Go home and rest. And ice will keep the swelling down. And for Pete's sake, don't anger any more policemen."

"Pass a message to Ms. Terry for me?" I said.

She clasped my free hand in hers and she squeezed. "Mr. August. You'll get hurt if you keep this up. My stars, hurt worse."

"Better me than someone else." I stood. It'd be more effective if the national anthem played but it didn't. My mangled face sold the show, though. "Tell her I'm still on the case. I'm looking for Caleb James. And I'm getting to the truth of what happened that night. Tell her, Sally."

I walked out the door and the movement made my head hurt.

## 24

Ronnie owned a blue cooling mask for cosmetic purposes and she put it in the fridge for me. Afterward I lay on the couch with the mask on my face, and it was too cold but it would help my face look less of a bruised potato.

She was ready for scorched earth. Raze Court Street down to cinders, string up the patrolmen as lanterns and set them on fire. Attach the police chief to the front of a truck and use him as a snowplow. Or the legal equivalent.

It would be tough to prove, I pointed out, and the circus would take away from my current investigation. And make me look like a sissy.

Seeking justice doesn't make one a sissy. That's obtuse, she said.

I didn't say I wouldn't get justice, I explained. But not yet. My hands were full at the moment.

And besides, I continued, I had baited them.

That is inconsequential, she said.

Not to me, I said.

Ronnie eventually grew frustrated with me and my Cro-Magnon tendencies and she took Kix to bed. Alone, I tried listening to Washington Nationals baseball but they'd sold their entire roster—except the bad expensive players, hooray—and listening to these strangers strikeout made me feel worse so I pushed buttons on the remote until the sound stopped.

Stackhouse returned.

She didn't speak and I didn't open my eyes but the person made sounds commensurate with Stackhouse—a keyring with too many keys, the creak of a leather belt releasing, work boots pushed off, a bottle of wine unstoppered, more wine poured than Timothy would. She sat beside me and she made a feminine grunt with the release of weight. A puff of air, the hint of perfume.

"Jake Robertson called me." When Stackhouse spoke, she sounded like Demi Moore—raspy, everything more sensual than she intended. "Told me my favorite boy fell over in his office, knocked himself unconscious. He didn't see it happen, but that you should be more careful."

"I'm your favorite boy?"

"Timothy," she said, "is my favorite man."

"And Manny?"

"Too pretty for me, babe. And he's too trim. With boobs like these," she said and I heard her pat herself, "you need a man with more meat on his bones."

"I don't see the correlation."

"You're not a woman."

"What'd you tell the chief?" I said.

"I told Jake that if my favorite boy ever fell down in his office again, he would spend a month in my jail with his badge lodged in his ass."

"You can't do that," I said.

"I didn't say I'd do it legally."

"See, you get it. Explain this to Ronnie."

A pause. She took a long throaty sip from her glass. Placed her hand on my shoulder and rubbed it, like one does a good dog. "Babe. You pissed them off on purpose."

"Probably."

"How'd you do it?"

"I told the prosecutor I knew Ervin Lane had been drunk and that they were covering it up, and if they didn't cooperate I'd tell the world."

She stopped rubbing my shoulder. I missed it.

"Babe."

"It worked, didn't it."

"Worked like a snowball throwing itself into hell," she said. "Could've gotten you shot."

"They don't strike me as accurate."

She said *Jesus* under her breath and started rubbing again. "Why'd you threaten them? And don't tell me only to help catch a damn fugitive. It's more than that."

Her question was good. And insightful, enough so it made my bruised brain hurt. I took a moment to marshal my resources.

"I'm mad at them. That's why."

"Because they're covering for Ervin," she said. "Mack, you were a cop. A lot of cops drink, often on the job. And they take care of their own. I wouldn't call it corruption, otherwise we're all corrupt."

"There aren't many corrupt cops."

"I concur."

"But when they're in a pack? It's a terrorist regime. They blamed the whole thing on a man addicted to meth."

"He deserves the blame," she said.

"He does. But not all of it."

"Didn't they cut him a good deal? The cop-killer got

thirty years instead of capital murder. He could be there for life. Or the chair," she said.

"I'm not saying Caleb didn't get what he deserved. I'm saying, there's more blame to go around, and I don't like the, 'Us innocent angels gotta catch that guilty bastard,' speeches I'm hearing."

"Because the girl got shot too," said Stackhouse.

"They're ducking their own culpability. It's hypocritical and maddening. Kim Harper died and they're spending their energy screaming how innocent they are. And..." Gingerly I took the cold mask off my face because it'd warmed and because the pressure hurt. She made a whistling sound, which I took to be a good sign. "And I'm angry for another reason. This is the first stimulating case in a while I have no chance of solving."

"You can't find Caleb."

"He could be anywhere. He could be in Des Moines, or San Diego, or Mexico, or Bum Country Nowhere, and I'll never find him. The marshals are tracking phones, and they set up cameras, and they're calling leads I don't know about, and they sent his picture to a thousand offices. They're good at this. And all I'm doing is, I'm running around pissing people off."

I heard a smile. "You're great, babe, at that."

"Probably I'm figuring out what happened that night, the night of the arrest, as a way of compensating. I can't find Caleb, and I know I can't, but at least I'll straighten out this other crooked thing."

"You mean," said Stackhouse, "you'll expose a pack of delinquent police officers in Lynchburg."

"Something like that."

"And get yourself shot."

"Hopefully not too hard," I said.

"Didn't you meet Ervin Lane and come away impressed? He's going to AA and turning his whole damn life around?"

"Yeah." I grinned. Ouch. "His prosthesis is big and clunky. He doesn't have a hook or a metallic thing attached to the socket. It's thick rubber and he can shove a bucket handle into its grasp."

"Why the hell are you grinning about that?"

"Because I like it. It's ugly but he isn't complaining. Just working. He's working a small farm and a job as a custodian at night, and he's trying to make a new beginning. No complaints. He even forgave the man who blew off his hand."

"And you want, what? You want him behind bars too? Because he'd been drinking?"

"No," I said.

"Then what?"

"Stackhouse." I did two snorts but they didn't help. In fact they hurt. "I don't know."

"You don't know."

"Correct. I don't know what the best outcome is. I can't see it yet. But I'm walking in the best direction I know."

She drank some wine.

"This is the first I can remember you admitting you're unsure of yourself."

"Is it sexy?" I said. "I'm hoping being vulnerable and lost is sexy."

"God no. Does Ronnie think it's sexy?"

"She does not."

Stackhouse stood and it sounded like she was stretching. She spoke the first words in a tight voice, then in a sigh, releasing some pressure.

"Mack. Kid. Don't make this more complex and difficult than it has to be. A meth addict shot a cop and you were hired to catch him. Don't get lost in all the collateral, because that's a deep, endless well of pain."

"I traffic in collateral," I said.

"Your face's purple."

"You hush," I said.

The front door opened and Manny strode in. He wore a backpack and carried a leather overnight bag in his left hand. He looked at me. At Stackhouse. Back at me.

"Ay, *amigaso*, I leave for a couple days and…" He pointed at me with his free hand. "And your face turns inside out?"

I frowned and winced and stopped frowning. "I'm vulnerable and lost and sexy."

Stackhouse laughed.

"Welcome home, babe."

Manny dropped the satchel and cocked his head.

"Your face might be better this way."

"You hush."

## 25

I looked like a car wreck so I spent Thursday morning in the office, not out in public. Kix had refused to speak to me and I saw no reason to scare more children. Even GPA stayed in the far corner, watching me from the side of her eye in case I morphed further into a monster from *Stranger Things*, her favorite show.

Today's agenda—find Robin.

Robin Lucas, the homie-hopper, potential mother of Caleb's baby, teacher gone missing. I'd emailed her but received no reply. She'd been involved with both men, and she could be the key I needed.

The last trace I had was Robin teaching elementary school in Halifax. Where'd she go afterward? I could ask her parents but they might take a look at my face and call the police and I hated those guys—they hit me when I wasn't looking. I could drive to Halifax and poke around—Robin would've needed childcare for her kid. Was the baby a secret? Caleb's dad thought so.

I was googling her and coming up empty, and I was rehearsing another call to Alethia Ramsay, her friend from the Halifax elementary school, asking if Robin had a kid, and who the childcare was, when my phone rang. Unknown number.

When I answered, Robin Lucas introduced herself.

*Zounds.*

Fortune favors the handsome.

Robin spoke in a rush, forcing out all the words she'd practiced. "I received your email, Mr. August. I can't help you. I don't know where Caleb is, and I wouldn't tell you if I did, because I believe he's innocent and the manhunt should be called off. Leave him alone and leave me alone." Some Lynchburg women sounded as though they'd taken speech therapy from Dolly Parton. Robin didn't—no country slang. Her message delivered, she softened. "No offense."

"You gotta work harder than that to offend me."

"If you insist."

"I'm his best chance, Robin."

She waited several heartbeats.

"Mr. August, you said you're on Caleb's side. You said no one else is but you. Yet you're trying to catch him."

"Caleb has little chance of evading capture indefinitely. And I won't help him do it. But he's got a puncher's chance of getting a reduced sentence, which is my purview."

"How can I believe that?"

"We could video conference so you can see my face."

"How would that help?"

"Because the Lynchburg police beat the hell out of me for trying to help Caleb. I look like I got stepped on," I said.

She said something under her breath about police officers.

"Who beat you up?"

"Guy named Whiteside and his friends," I said, and she mirthlessly laughed.

"I know Jonas Whiteside. He's been a bully his whole life. He tried to rape my little sister when they were teenagers. They aren't all bad, the Lynchburg police, but there's an amoral strain. Including Jonas." A noisy sigh in my ear. "I'm confused. You're trying to catch Caleb, ostensibly helping the police. But they're angry with you. So... What am I missing?"

"My pursuit of Caleb threatens to expose them."

"What'd they do?"

"Great question. Wish I knew for sure," I said. "Robin, the marshals will catch him. And his life will be worse than it was before he broke out. If he works with me, it might be better."

"What about Ervin?"

"What about him?" I said, and I detected a little something. I didn't know what. But something. A little of it.

"You mentioned exposing the Lynchburg police. Would they, um, arrest Ervin?"

"That's not my intent. There's a lot of blame to go around. And maybe Ervin already paid enough."

"If you ask me, Mr. August, they've both paid enough. And you should leave them be."

I stood and paced my office. GPA's eyes rolled to follow me. Walking across the space, I passed through a blast of cold air issued from the A/C vent. The far side of the office was warm, and I passed through the cold zone again on my return trip.

"Tell me the story, Robin."

"Which story?"

"Of you and Ervin and Caleb."

"That is not your business," she said.

"A barista blabbed that you're a homie-hopper."

She made a groan. I knew from her photos that she was thin and good-looking. Was she still? Was her hair still long and straight? Had the past couple years worn her out and she'd quit hiking to care for the baby? I wasn't a hundred percent positive the baby existed.

I gave her time.

"Mr. August." When she spoke she did so with a tremor. "I made straight As in high school. I never missed church. I babysat and saved the money to buy a car. I was on Heritage's homecoming court, and I've never done drugs. I didn't drink until I was twenty-one, and I..." She made a rustling noise and I thought she was wiping her face. "I did life the best I knew how, and what happens? Baristas are telling strangers that I'm a homie-hopper. What a *ridiculous* expression."

"You dated Ervin Lane."

"I dated Ervin Lane. The biggest mistake of my life. And I'm still paying the price. You can do everything correctly and precisely, Mr. August, and then in a moment of weakness... One decision, and everything changes. I'm sure that's how Caleb feels too."

Still I paced the office. The movement gave me something to do, so I wasn't stationary with a pulsing face.

"Tell me who the real Caleb is, Robin. On one hand, he impressed a prison librarian enough to secure his escape. He offered to pay for Marky's rehab. On the other hand, there's rumors he stole from a large investment firm in New York. There's video of him attacking guards at the Lynchburg jail. And of course he resisted arrest that night and shot Kim Harper."

"I told you, Mr. August. One decision and everything changes."

"That's a series of decisions, not one."

"That's not what I meant," she said. "Caleb's bad decision happened in New York. He was like me, in many ways. He came from a good family. He went to church too. He was the valedictorian. But then, during his internship, he caved to the pressure."

"Cocaine."

"He was hooked like *that*." I heard her snap. "When he came home…"

"Crystal meth."

"Yes," she said. "He didn't *want* to be an addict."

"You didn't detect it immediately," I said.

"Not at first, no."

"You were with Ervin Lane at the time. But you rekindled the romance with Caleb on the side?"

"Mr. August…" She laughed some, and I found myself liking her more and more. She was composed and well spoken, even as I badgered her. "I don't know who your sources are, but they're good."

"Church gossip is a powerful thing," I said.

"*Oh*. Of course. The Baptists and the Presbyterians and the Episcopalians smiling and singing hymns while clawing each other's eyes out. It was denominational bickering that killed Christ."

"That's the way I read it too. We're still white-washed tombs, aren't we."

"You've read the New Testament," she said.

"It sounds to me like Caleb and Ervin have forgiven each other, which is nice. But that doesn't mean the marshals won't catch him."

"They haven't yet."

"Where'd you go after you left Halifax?" I said.

"That is not your business, either."

"Your baby," I said, taking a risk. "Is that why you had to leave town?"

"I..."

"Is it Caleb's? Is that why he was desperate to get out of prison?"

—click—

The call ended.

Rats.

Double rats.

"Mackenzie, you ass," I said.

I typed a text and sent it.

**Robin. That was pushing too far, and I apologize. Please tell Caleb I can get him a better deal. Call me back and we'll discuss.**

I waited.

No response. Some sort of fishing metaphor lurked in my mind, about reeling in a fish but getting impatient and losing it.

Triple rats.

## 26

Noelle Beck graced my office at lunch. Manny accompanied her. She plugged my cell phone into her laptop and did wizard things with it.

"No luck," she determined. "Robin's phone isn't registered with any major service provider so we can't track her with CSLI. I tried pinging her device but it failed." Noelle made a light sucking sound at her teeth, peering into her screen, tapping keys. "This is an odd telephone number. My guess is, she called you with a computer program that went through her internet connection, specifically so we couldn't trace her."

Manny stood behind her, arms crossed, watching her work. The two of them were aware of the other at all times. As Noelle worked, she did so with the knowledge that Manny watched her, and he watched her knowing she knew it. She wore a skirt she would've died before wearing three years ago.

Existing around Manny was hard. I knew from experience, those who wandered into his orbit were buffeted by the gravity. Most simply couldn't be themselves. His accent was too much like Antonio Banderas', his hair too perfect, he smelled too good, his waist too small, his eyes too bright, *something*. Noelle Beck held up far better than most, but she wanted his approval the same way everyone else did.

The only difference with her was, she had his approval. And he wanted hers in return, which he got, much of the time, but was it enough?

A dance with scruples and professionalism and lust and desire and the first person to cave lost.

Noelle still wore no engagement ring.

She had spoken to me and I missed it, lost in thoughts of mutual love unrequited.

"I said, I'll keep working on Robin's phone, but no promises."

"Thanks, Noelle," I said.

"This information." Manny nodded toward my phone. "Robin's phone call. We don't tell Lynchburg. *Pendejos*."

Noelle closed her laptop. "I'll leave that decision to you, Manny."

"I decided," he said. "*Vamanos?*"

"When you're ready."

"I'm ready." He opened the office door for her and she said goodbye to me and they left as one, moving more closely than Manny and I ever did.

GPA looked at me with concern.

I returned the look.

"I adjure you, Georgina, by the gazelles of the field, do not awaken love until she pleases," I told her.

*What?*

"I don't know," I said.

The stairs were still creaking with their descent when someone new darkened my door.

I had a visitor. Sally Gardner, Elaine Terry's matronly receptionist.

I'd been expecting her.

She was staring open-mouthed down the stairwell. The door closed, and Manny and Beck were gone, and Sally came into my office.

"Mr. August," she said. "Are those friends of yours?"

"Friends and colleagues. Aren't I lucky."

"My stars. That may be the most beautiful man I've ever laid eyes on. And so..." She made a shivering motion and it wasn't from the air conditioned blast. "And the girl was lovely too, even though she needs to fasten a few buttons on her blouse."

"Agree to disagree."

"Do you have a spell to gossip?" said Sally.

"Please come in and have a seat. I haven't eaten yet and I'll order us lunch."

"Oh my stars." Sally laughed. I was a riot. "Thank you, Mr. August, but no. I've packed my lunch for twenty years without missing a day."

"What's it like to be salt of the earth, Mrs. Gardner? Is it empowering?"

"I don't know about that." She sat in the client chair I offered, and I sat in the other. This was no time to be removed across a desk from her, like we weren't best of pals. Pals who shared secrets.

"What can I do for you?"

"Your face looks..." She made a polite but pitiful expression. "Well, God bless it."

"The next day is always bad. But tomorrow, though, it'll be yellow. Hooray."

She nodded. Her back was straight and her hands were on her knees. She wore another flowery dress that reached her shoes, flat on the floor, some kind of covered leather sandal. Something loomed in her mind but she needed to work up to it.

"Your office is, um…"

"Masculine?" I said.

"I would say, functional?"

"Spartan?

"What does Spartan mean?" she said.

"Like a Spartan would use it."

"Oh," she said, like I wasn't a riot. "The potpourri is nice."

"Thank you. Not enough people notice. This blend is called Gun Smoke and Vengeance."

"Is it really?"

"Depends on if you ask me or the manufacturer."

"Either way. It suits."

I smiled winsomely. "How's Elaine?"

"She's taking depositions in Richmond, so I took a personal day. My first in three years."

"I'm honored."

"After yesterday…" She kinda winced at my face. "After you came in, Mr. August, I spent the evening thinking."

"I spent the evening groaning."

"I'm sure you did." Another wince. "I hate that it happened to you, Mr. August. I hate that it was Lynchburg police. I hate that it was over a case that Ms. Elaine Terry…"

"Not your fault, Sally."

"No. But… It's the fault of someone. It's the fault of a system that I'm… Not complicit, but that I'm a part of, I suppose you could say." Her hands fussed with the dress around her knees. "That's the devil of it."

"Sacrifices must be made. And I'm willing."

Georgina Princess rolled her eyes.

Sally did too.

"I know what you're doing, Mr. August," she said.

"What's that?"

"You want me to feel pity for you."

"Is it working?" I said.

She looked away, at my desk. "I have worked for Ms. Terry for twelve years. She paid for my licensure as a paralegal. When my papa died, she came to the funeral. And in the family I was raised, loyalty is a highly prized thing."

"If you help me, you could be fired. But even worse than that..."

She took off her glasses to dab at her eyes with a tissue she snatched from the box on my desk.

I said, "You'd feel like you betrayed someone."

"She's a hard woman. She can be cold. But she has been professionally courteous, Mr. August. She's been loyal. And she's Lynchburg." She paused to sniff and pinch at her nose with the tissue. "I worked in that office before she arrived. She inherited me, if that makes sense to you. The man before her... Well. The plainest way to put it, I suppose, is that there are levels to integrity."

"Who was before her?"

"Man by the name of Tim Beckett. A gentleman. He practiced in that house for twenty-five years, and I never once caught him in a lie or an unwholesome compromise, no sir. He retired and half the town came out. Very unlike... Well. Things change, don't they." She smiled, sad and bittersweet in her memories.

"Elaine compromises."

"Ms. Terry's father was a police officer in Lynchburg." Sally nodded to herself. "Like a lot of them, he got testicular cancer from the radar guns, you know. Had to retire early, but he still volunteers as a resource officer at Linkhorne, like a lot of the old guard do, since all the gun violence in the news. Ms. Terry was raised to protect Lynchburg. And sometimes, I hate to say it, that means she doesn't put her client first."

"She puts Lynchburg first," I said.

"The thing I can't stop thinking about, Mr. August, was that this case was rotten from the beginning. Rotten as a bad apple."

"I think so too."

"And this time around, maybe, just maybe, Lynchburg would be better off if it weren't protected, if you understand me."

"I do, in fact," I said.

"If I show you something, Mr. August, you have to give me your word. *Promise* me that you'll keep me a secret."

"You were never here."

"And we never spoke a word and I never showed you a thing," said Sally.

"Not a single thing."

She sniffed again and dabbed at her eyes and put her glasses back on. "As Ms. Terry's office manager, I have access to her files. And I thought maybe..." A deep shaky breath. "I thought you might benefit from seeing the video taken from the dash camera of Ervin Lane's police car. I have it here on my phone."

"Chief Robertson showed me the video, but I'd like to examine it more closely."

A sad smile from Sally.

"The video I brought, Mr. August, hasn't been doctored. The video you watched was, I'd bet my life."

"Jiminy Christmas, Ms. Gardner," I said.

Her smile grew sadder. "I think I might've destroyed my whole career with those words."

"What words? I heard you say nothing," I said.

Chief Robertson's video had been doctored, that old sly dog. And I didn't catch it.

She removed her phone from a pocket in her dress and held it out to me with a shaking hand.

"It's ready. Press play," she said. "And may God forgive me."

I swiped my thumb across the screen and it unlocked. There was the queued video.

I pressed play.

The same distorted jumpy screen, the same white BMW 3, the same flashing shades of blue.

"Louder, Mr. August," she said.

I thumbed up the volume.

Ervin was talking at the BMW's window.

I still couldn't hear the words but there was ambient sound.

While we watched the silent conversation at the BMW, I asked Sally, "Ervin used to be a detective. Why is he no longer?"

"That was some juicy gossip, I can tell you. Ervin arrived to court drunk. Twice. You never saw Judge Brown so furious. Mr. Robertson had to demote him, or whatever the term is."

On screen, Kim Harper eased into view. The right side of the phone.

Caleb stood out of the car. Pale and thin, whereas Ervin bulged at his uniform.

I could hear them now, screaming at each other.

So far this looked identical to the video Robertson played.

I didn't want to watch Kim Harper die again.

The men started wrestling. Shoving, punching. Caleb's

ineffective, Ervin's thunderous. Caleb slipping free, Ervin grabbing at his shirt.

Caleb screaming, *Let go, let go, Ervin, let me goooo.*

They moved off screen. Kim Harper was shouting into her shoulder.

—*Squad eighteen, driver engaged with Officer Lane! 10-33, I need backup.*

—*Copy squad eighteen, Officer Lane engaged. All cars, 10-33 on Hollins Mill.*

Then she stopped.

*There.*

Something was different. An indefinable wrong. Not immediately obvious. I didn't know... I watched her, my pulse in my ears.

What changed?

Kim Harper staring, not talking into her radio.

Kim Harper still staring...

BOOM.

She took a bullet to the throat. She clutched at her collar and fell into the BMW's glaring headlights.

"Ugh," I said.

"Isn't it awful."

Harper's face was hidden behind the BMW.

Caleb ran into the screen.

This was new. Robertson had stopped it before I saw this.

Caleb's screams were picked up by the interior camera. *Hey! HEY! Help, oh my God, HELP HELP!*

Poor Kim Harper squirming. Caleb's face was a sheen of pallid sweat, bright in the headlights. He fumbled with her radio, still shouting, but the shoulder receiver was partially pinned under her.

"He doesn't remember any of this," I said.

Caleb tore off his shirt. A white business shirt. He pressed the shirt into her neck, and he was crying, and I could hear some of it. I felt like crying too.

Ervin reappeared.

Despite the video quality, something was clearly wrong with Ervin's left wrist. He kept the arm tight to his body. Using his free hand, Ervin cuffed Caleb in the head, knocking him over. Knocking him away from Kim Harper.

No wonder Robertson didn't want me to see this. Caleb was trying to save Kim's life. And Ervin—

Caleb scrambled away, back to Kim, screaming, *Stop STOP you fucking IDIOT*, back to his shirt, to the officer it was far too late to save.

Ervin grabbed him again. I had to give Ervin a modicum of credit—his hand was dangling useless and he was bleeding out, but still he persisted in his arrest. Ervin pinned Caleb against thin grass, using his remaining good hand to hit Caleb in the back of the head. We could only partially view this, some of it hidden by the BMW.

—*Squad nine on site. Looks like officer down.*

Two more cops darted into view. Finally. One guy stopped at Kim, one guy ran to help Ervin.

—*Officer down on Hollins Mill! Oh God. Officer down, request ambulance! Shit, it's Kim.*

The guy helping Ervin, he took Caleb's shirt off the ground and did something with it, couldn't see, maybe making a tourniquet. The officer with Kim Harper, his hands were black and glinting with her blood.

Caleb wasn't moving. He'd passed out, full of shock and adrenaline and methamphetamines.

The video ended and I had to remember where I was.

Sally held my box of tissues, and I took one.

"Breaks my heart each time, Mr. August."

I stood and set the phone on my desk. I paced my office twice, getting the icy blast from the vents. Outside a man was playing a banjo on the corner of Jefferson. I'd seen him before, playing with his case open for tips until he was run off by the manager of the American National Bank.

Shake it off, Mackenzie. Earn it.

I paced the office space again, sat, and picked up her phone. Used my finger to skip the video backward and I watched it again.

BMW.

Ervin and his flashlight.

Shouting. Kim on screen.

Caleb stood out. Fighting. Radio.

*10-33, I need backup!*

Off screen. Kim watching.

BOOM.

Kim falls. Caleb rushing to her.

No, dammit, I'd already missed the discrepancy. What had been altered? I scrubbed the video backward and watched again.

Sally silently let me work. Maybe she knew the answer, maybe she didn't, but she didn't talk and I was grateful.

BMW. Ervin. Kim. Caleb. Shouting. BOOM. She fell.

Again.

Ervin. Caleb. Off-screen. BOOM. Kim.

Again.

BOOM. Kim.

Again.

BOOM.

The hazy thing in the back of my mind snapped into focus.

"Oh," I said. "Oh man."

Sally nodded.

"Jiminy Christmas." I set the phone down like it was hot.

That's what initially bothered me when I viewed the fight in Robertson's office—Kim Harper showed no reaction to the first gunshot.

*Because it was nonexistent.*

"You heard the difference, Mr. August?"

"I did," I said. "There's only one gunshot. In Robertson's, there are two gunshots. Kim was struck by the second bullet." I stood up and walked the office again. "Someone layered in the sound of a second gunshot. That's why Kim seemed unfazed. Why the hell'd they add a second? They added it..." I closed my eyes to think. "They added a gunshot *before* the one that hit Kim. When I watched it, Robertson talked about the first gunshot. The nonexistent bullet. He said, '*There*, he shot Ervin's hand off.'"

"Did he? The devil."

"But that wasn't true. Caleb hadn't fired yet. So why'd Robertson...?"

"I'm afraid I don't know, Mr. August. I don't know what happened. All I know is that Ms. Elaine Terry is good with altering videos. She has a program on her computer that does it. I forget the name. But Ms. Terry neglected to delete the original version in our shared folder," said Sally.

Elaine Terry was involved in the cover-up.

A corrupt lawyer. Wonders never cease.

I paced more and I talked out loud.

"Only one gunshot. Means the single bullet passed through Ervin's hand and hit Kim." The banjo kept playing as I pictured the action in my mind. I used my hands like I was wrestling with Ervin. Then like I was wrestling with Caleb. "Only one gunshot. Caleb fires at Ervin, hits him below the palm, catches Kim..." I turned, eyes still closed, like I was Caleb, facing Kim, Ervin in my way, and I held the gun. Envisioning the scene like I was there. BMW, flashing blue emergency lights, scrubby grass. "I've got the gun and I'm aiming at Ervin... Ervin is between me and Kim... He's... What is he doing, he's running at me? Are we still wrestling? Did I get free from him? How'd I get the gun?"

"I wouldn't know, Mr. August."

"I'm Caleb, I'm thin, I can't outwrestle Ervin. I couldn't fight him for the gun and win. Which means I took it from his holster, before he knew what was happening. Right?"

Sally didn't speak.

I continued, my eyes closed.

"I grabbed it out of Ervin's holster. But. No. Ervin wore his duty holster. Designed to prevent unauthorized withdrawals. Facing Ervin, the holster would prevent me from withdrawing it. So... Was I behind him? How'd I withdraw his pistol?" I was standing in the cold blast, though I felt my blood hot. "If we're wrestling for it, how'd I... He's too big. We're separated by a few feet? No, Ervin wouldn't let go of me. Right? Did I get behind him and pull the pistol? We're fighting... Kim watching. Kim talking into her radio, then she stops. She's watching us. She's watching us fight for the gun. Just watching us? That makes no sense. If I have the gun, and we're fighting... But what if I don't have the gun? What if Ervin has the gun? What if Ervin has the gun..." Eyes closed, still kinda wrestling with my hands, I'm there, drunk Ervin breathing on me. Ervin has the gun, not me, maybe I'm trying to get it, maybe he... But if he has the gun... He's drunk, he's screaming, red in the face, he has the gun...

BOOM.

One gunshot.

Caleb running into the picture, screaming for help.

Using his shirt.

Running into the picture, not holding a pistol.

Because he never had it.

*Only one gunshot.*

I walked to my chair and sat down. Lowered my head into my hands and told myself, "Wow."

"Mr. August?"

"That's why they added the second gunshot. They wanted it to look like Caleb had the gun and he was shooting at both cops. But he wasn't."

"I don't understand what you mean."

I drew in air. Held it. Thought it through again. Pinched my lips, let the air out through my nose. Which hurt.

"Caleb never had the gun. Ervin had it. Ervin drew it and accidentally blew off his own hand and killed Kim Harper," I said, and Sally made a gasp. "Caleb didn't shoot either of them. Ervin killed Kim. That's what they're covering up. I'm chasing an innocent fugitive."

"Oh my stars, I just *knew* something was rotten!"

"The Boonsboro Baptist Sunday school class is going to be furious."

## 27

That night after dinner I presented my case to a captive audience. A captive and powerful audience, which I'd need to take down a corrupt regime. Ronnie Summers, feared litigator. Stackhouse, a respected sheriff. Manny Martinez, federal marshal. And Timothy August, elementary principal, who grew squeamish during the video and left, upstairs to take a shower, and I didn't blame him.

They watched the video on my phone and I explained the doctored version. Then, using Manny, I acted out what I deduced happened off-screen. Manny portrayed Caleb, and I the drunk arresting officer. During our tussle, I pulled my imaginary service pistol. I had hold of Manny by the shirt collar. I aimed at him and I was drunk and we were fighting and I missed, hitting my own hand instead, the hand holding Manny's collar, and then striking Kim Harper beyond.

I (Ervin) fell to the ground, leaving Manny upright to run help the wounded Kim Harper, until I lumbered to arrest him, ignoring my fallen sister-in-arms.

Reviewing the facts later that night, Chief Robertson

had made the call—this could never reach the public. Especially not after Kim was shot by a cop already busted for drunkenness on the job. He and Ervin would never survive the ensuing tsuris.

Manny said if I tried to explain what tsuris meant he would hit me in my tender nose with his shoe, so I carried on.

They concocted a plan to blame it all on Caleb, who, to be fair, had resisted arrest and looked like a wild man on the video. A perfect scapegoat.

How deep did the corruption go? I bet not far. The more people who knew, the greater the chance of exposure. Chief Robertson knew and Elaine Terry knew, the old Lynchburg guard, conspiring over the years to cover a multitude of sins. The inner circle.

However, there must be a second layer of trustees who were told a partial truth, that Ervin had been drinking but Caleb was the real killer. That a good defense attorney could use Ervin's inebriation against them, possibly getting the murderous wicked cop-killing Caleb off the charges, which couldn't be allowed to happen. This second layer of trustees might involve officer Whiteside and his goons, and the prosecutor Terrance Goodwin (who was new to Lynchburg), and maybe even the judge. Small towns were good at circling the wagons for the greater good.

Let's put the murderous wicked cop killer away quickly. Let's cut him a good deal so he'll plead and this entire headache vanishes.

Tomorrow Ronnie would arrange for subpoenas. Then Saturday, when Robertson would likely be out of the office, we'd descend apace on evidence lockers and police documents. If Robertson and Elaine were willing to doctor the video, then they'd be willing to tamper with the police report and other evidence, like the gun. The original video was enough but I wanted additional ammunition, proof of their fraudulence, enough that Sally might not be suspected as the source, enough that Internal Affairs wouldn't blink at backing us.

"You're forgetting something, Mackenzie," said Ronnie.

My case made, weary, I sat down. "I do not forget."

"Someone else is in the inner circle. Ervin Lane," she said.

I hadn't forgotten him. I only didn't want to think about him yet.

"That's right, babe. You're crazy about the guy," said Stackhouse. "He moved out west and turned his life around, like Pa Ingalls. You said he's sober and doing great, even with one hand. One big ugly rubber hand only good for carrying a bucket, but he's trying anyway. And you're going to ruin his new life."

Ervin Lane on his little farm, a pastoral Eden, feeding the chickens. Serving me lemonade. Careful not to drop things with his one hand, the hand he didn't blow off with a Glock. Ervin looking into the distance, telling me he'd forgiven Caleb, to please leave Caleb alone.

A pink heart in the window. Some lucky lady in town who'd hit the jackpot with this former cop, retired, tattooed, a kind man now. Losing weight, driving his truck to AA meetings, no longer the angry drunk.

"To prove Caleb's innocent," said Ronnie, "you'll ruin Ervin's life."

"Must we?"

"Who's this we?" said Manny. "You're the *hombre* gonna ruin the cop's life, guy with only one hand, not me."

"Caleb will no longer be the wanted man," Ronnie said.

"It'll be Ervin. Which is how it should be, according to that video."

All of a sudden, the words of Robin Lucas floated back.

*If you ask me, Mr. August, they've both paid enough. And you should leave them be.*

I wasn't sure I could do that.

---

## 28

Ronnie's office was located off Salem Avenue in a renovated brick two-story building near the train yard. A modernized, vogue spot, where cool kids plied their trade. She worked on the second story in her boutique private firm behind a handsome and heavy wooden door. Her white baseboards and crown molding were tall and the walls were painted a trendy pale blue, and the place looked designed to be the office of a feel-good-movie's plucky young up-and-coming heroine boss babe.

Ronnie wanted to expand. She'd been threatening to for a while, but recently she'd ramped the intensity, and she needed more space if she was to hire a couple fresh-faced attorneys. We sat side-by-side on the little couch, dreaming about the future, about a different office, about what could be. I was also dreaming about how to get her shirt off, but she had meetings at the courthouse soon about getting subpoenas for the Lynchburg shooting, and before that a zoom, so it probably wasn't the right time to chase my dreams.

Charlotte Andrews knocked on the front door and

called, "Knock knock, anyone *home*?" and Ronnie's receptionist Katie Drake greeted her. Ronnie stood from the
couch and they hugged like women do, differently than men
do, and Charlotte apologized for coming by without an
appointment.

Charlotte Andrews, Ronnie's childhood friend, seeking a
divorce from her baby's father because he'd sold his two
restaurants and was using his newfound autonomy to write
a novel.

I knew enough about women's shoes to know Charlotte's
heeled sandals were expensive, and so was her green Coach
bag. Her flat-front khakis and sleeveless blouse looked
formally fashionable, now out-of-date and tight. She knew it
and wore the shame of it, compensating with energy. The
shame was self-imposed and worsened by her comparison
to Ronnie, and Ronnie knew it and tried to put her at ease
by mentioning the good handbag and her modish hairstyle
—short, chin length, bangs kinda like Audrey Hepburn.

"What happened to your face?" Charlotte asked me.

"Walrus."

"*Walrus*?"

"Walrus." Us good detectives always repeat stuff.

"*Okaaay*. Don't tell me. Well. Today's one of the mornings I get to dump Ethan off at childcare and be an adult."
Charlotte closed her eyes and smiled with the catharsis. "Sit
at a coffee shop and scroll Instagram and read magazines
and fall in love with myself again. Care to join, Ron?"

"I wish I could. I'm booked solid." Ronnie smiled at her
and I'd never get over how good her teeth were. Like little
piano keys if little piano keys had sex appeal. "Besides,
whenever I spend time with only myself, I fall farther out of
love with her."

"Oh Ron." Charlotte laughed and *laughed*. "With a body

like that, I'd spend the day in front of the mirror. God, one day I'll have it back. One day. Then we'll go out dancing."

I eased toward the door.

"No no, don't go," Charlotte cooed. "I'm not interrupting, only need quick legal advice. Would you advise I stay off Tinder?"

"Yes," I said.

"Not *your* advice, handsome," said Charlotte.

"Tinder, the dating app?" Ronnie said.

"That's the one!" Charlotte clenched her fists, like she'd grabbed something heavy. "I'm eager for a man. A *real* man."

"Charlotte, sweetie, I've been procrastinating on our phone call. I needed to tell you. I can't be your attorney," said Ronnie.

Charlotte's fervor deflated like she'd been popped.

"*What!* Why not? What happened? You're the *best*."

Ronnie leaned backwards on her desk, kinda sitting on it. "Because I don't think you should leave him."

Charlotte blinked.

"You're not allowed to say that."

"To a random client, I wouldn't. But you're not. You're Charlotte Andrews and I love you," said Ronnie.

"You're a divorce attorney."

"I'm your friend first."

"Well *don't* be," said Charlotte. "Why shouldn't I divorce him?"

"Because it's bad for you, sweetie."

"It's *bad* for me." Charlotte spat the word bad and the word bad fell on the ground like a bag of concrete. I really wanted to leave. "What the hell does that mean, Ron?"

"Does your husband hit you?"

"Of course not. Though he'd like to, some days," said Charlotte.

"Is he emotionally cruel?"

"I don't know. He quit his *job*, Ron."

"Did he abandon you?"

"No, he's around *too* much. Far too fucking much," said Charlotte.

"Did he have an affair?"

"He'd like to do that too, I'm sure."

"Is he an involved father?" said Ronnie.

"Ron. Baby. You're not listening. He quit his job. He's listless, sitting at his computer, reading books, God, it's awful. Ethan and I are worn *out*."

Ronnie pressed her lips together and shook her head.

"These aren't grounds for divorce."

"*So what*? Do some lawyer shit. I'm not happy. What do you mean divorce will be bad for me?"

Ronnie looked into Charlotte and beyond her and she squinted, searching for the phrasing to sway the jury of one.

"I don't know how to explain it. It's an indefinable conviction, sweetie, that you'll be happier staying married."

"Oh my god," said Charlotte.

"And not only that, work on being a better wife."

Charlotte looked like she might die.

"Are you *kidding me*," said Charlotte. "You're the worst fucking divorce attorney I ever..."

"I know. I'm sorry for the bad news."

"This bullshit is easy for you to say." Charlotte waved a hand my direction. "You married the right one."

I shrugged modestly.

"He's not the right one. He's just a man," said Ronnie.

I took my shrug back.

"He makes me happy. But I'm the happiest when I'm a good wife," said Ronnie. "Not when he's a good husband."

"Wow," I said.

Ronnie closed her eyes and pinched at the bridge of her nose. "I know. I'm mortified that cornball shit came out of my mouth. But I believe it's true."

"This is..." said Charlotte. "This is... What the hell kinda feminist are you?"

"I'm still a feminist. But a feminist in love. One who has reached the end of feminism and found it incomplete."

"No. You're like a... I don't know what you are, but you're like a... He brainwashed you."

Ronnie's chin came up and her eyes did a flashing thing. It was scary and she wasn't even aimed at me.

"Charlotte. My father gave me *no* money for college, and yet here you are, standing in my law office. I'm a successful businesswoman. I make twice my husband's salary. Sometimes I hire him as a private contractor. My firm is ready to expand. I'm not the one seeking a divorce from my husband because he might no longer provide the lifestyle I cannot provide myself. I don't appreciate your insinuation. Trust me, I'm a feminist." Ronnie took a deep breath. "But before that, I'm a female. And a wife. And I'm fucking committed to it. What kind of example of a feminist would I be if I break my promises? If I'm a liar?"

Charlotte searched for some good words to use, for a rebuttal. If she'd been in court, she would've asked the judge for a short recess.

"But..." She did her best. "But I told you I'm not happy. I'm miserable."

"Yes I heard you."

"And your advice is, instead of getting a divorce, I should make my husband happy," said Charlotte.

"I said no such thing. What did I say?"

"I..."

"Did I say that, Mackenzie?" Ronnie was still flared with

anger. "Did I say she should focus on making her husband happy?"

"You didn't, but pretend I'm not here."

"I said you should work on being a better wife," said Ronnie.

"That's the *same thing*!" Charlotte cried.

"No it isn't. I don't know him, I don't care about him, not a single damn bit, sweetie. I care about you. And… based on my few years with Mackenzie, I can tell you that working on being a better wife will make you happier. That's what Mackenzie does, constantly improving himself, working on being a better husband, finding completeness in the work, and he's so damn happy and content some-times I want to hit him. I'm suggesting you do a selfish thing. Stop chasing your own happiness, because it's making you miserable."

Charlotte threw up her hands.

"That's absurd!"

"I know. It's upside down. But it works."

"When did you get so preachy?" said Charlotte. "No." She shook her head, gave a slight sneer. "No. Look at you. Those gorgeous legs, that tiny waist, you never birthed a child, your Botox and the hair… You don't get to judge me. You don't have the *right*."

"Your husband doesn't hurt you, he's around, you two share a child, and you made him a promise. I'm not judging, I'm predicting—divorce won't make you happy. You came for advice. Here it is. No, don't get on Tinder. You already swiped right, or whatever the hell it is. Now do your best. If your husband begins abuse, come back. Until then—"

"*Come back*. No fucking way am I *ever* coming back." Charlotte turned on her heel, the heel of her good expensive sandal, and left. She stomped, she stormed. She called,

"Bitch!" over her shoulder and she was gone, like a storm with a Coach bag.

Ronnie and I held our places, with no words. We couldn't see Katie Drake but I bet she was frozen too. If we remained still, Charlotte might not return.

She didn't.

Ronnie rolled her eyes.

"I did that poorly," she said.

"I object."

"I didn't want to say that tripe. I don't even know if it's true. It sounded so odd."

"The truth can be cumbersome," I said.

"But she has to grow up. She's believing lies." Ronnie made a long sigh. "Isn't she?"

"I think so. But I'm a man. Not the man, just a man."

"Ha ha." She pushed away from the desk and we hugged and I enjoyed her body against me. "I'd rather be shouted at by a judge than do that again. But I think I'm correct. I think she needs the work of growing up. It's hard but it's good." She was talking into my shoulder. "Growing up has been good for me. And her husband sounds like he bears her no ill will. I'm not sure how he puts up with her."

"No need to continue your defense. The arbitrator already decided in your favor."

"I'm sorry I said I wanted to hit you."

"Do you?" I asked.

"Sometimes. When you get preachy."

"I do not get preachy."

"Where do you think I learned it from?" she said.

"Careful. The arbitrator is on your side but it's now tenuous."

A smile in her voice. "I have no fear. The arbitrator is mad for me. He's biased."

"But also capable of making decisions in spite of his prurience."

We were still pressed together and she shifted her hips against mine.

"Is the arbitrator prurient now?" she said.

"Almost always."

"He's only biased because I wore high heels and I've been using $300 Le Mer body cream."

"For a lot of reasons," I said. "But the heels are dispositive."

"Would he like to have intimate congress if I close the door and we're quiet?"

"Did you say three hundred dollars?" I said.

Ronnie released me and stepped into her reception area and told Katie Drake to get some coffee and croissants and to take her time. Katie left quickly and Ronnie returned to me and she said, "Mackenzie. Don't focus on the cost. Focus on me."

"Three hundred dollars?"

"Mackenzie."

"You have a zoom soon," I told her.

"Me," she said. "Focus on me. Me, me, me."

We did.

But we both benefited.

## 29

Manny and I sat on the front porch in rocking chairs fixing the universe. We did this without speaking but it happened nonetheless.

One of the pleasant things about Roanoke was the absence of light pollution. The city produced some but it was like the earth glowed instead of the sky. The night was partially hidden by thick green leaves but what we could see of the cosmos twinkled smartly, the Milky Way indistinct but apparent, reminding us that we were insignificant and it was a good thing. I could feel people in their homes all around, and feel the loom of the city to the north, but these environs knew to remain soft and unobtrusive.

Manny'd had a date that night. Holly Waters, anchor of the local CBS news broadcast at noon. Holly had driven to our house, insisting on picking Manny up, insisting on driving him, which she thought would be fun and show her gumption. It doomed her from the start. Manny was the driver. You didn't force yourself on Manny. She'd tried winning him over the way she would a television audience, with power and pizzazz and appeal, but Manny wasn't a man to be won. He was a rock to shatter against.

He'd returned from the date two hours later in an Uber. Driving the Uber. The owner of the car rode in the passenger seat bewildered but bewitched.

Kix and I had been on the front porch when he returned. He walked past us into the kitchen, his boots angry. Came back with a margarita for himself, a margarita for me, and a juice for Kix. He sat in the opposite rocking chair and that's where we were now, silently fixing the universe, sipping a strong cocktail, Kix breathing deeply in my lap, me thankful for the work of growing up because it meant I no longer fought in cages Friday nights in Los Angeles, but rather rocked in chairs in a city with no light pollution.

Manny spoke after a long time.

"She's gonna tell that criminal *jefe* yes."

I deciphered. "Noelle Beck decided to marry Rocky, but she hasn't told him."

"Hard to say no to a billionaire."

"Did you give her a reason not to?" I said.

Kix asleep on my lap twisted to get more comfortable, and he muttered about wise stock investments. The night was warm and he sweated.

Manny drank some margarita. A low-carb margarita with fresh lime juice, a splash of agave, one squeezed orange, and a shocking amount of tequila.

"You can't," I said.

Manny shook his head. "I can't."

"Because you don't love her."

He made a noise like a grunt. No meaning behind it.

"Because you don't know if you can love anyone," I said.

Manny swirled the glass, ice tinkling.

"Love you and Ronnie and Kix. Probably as good as I can do," he said.

"You loved someone once. Love her like Michael Bolton says a man loves a woman."

"Catalina García. How'd that turn out, *amigo*?"

"You shot her," I said.

"Growing up like I did, you didn't love people. You used them. You survived them. Even your mom you hated, some days."

"Then you tried love in your twenties and it failed. Now you're you, and that's enough," I said.

"That's enough."

"Until it isn't."

He made another of the indiscernible grunts.

"Until Noelle gets married," I said.

"She shouldn't marry guys in a cartel."

"Whom should she?"

"No one. I'm good, she's good, everything's good," he said.

"What if she's not good?"

He peered into his glass and a muscle in his jaw worked. "I'm no solution to that. *Señorita* deserves... *No sé*. She's one of the great ones, Mack."

"She is."

"If she's not good... Don't know there's a *hombre* out there good enough to fix it."

"There isn't," I said. "But that's part of it. Two broken people who together form something closer to a whole. It's not enough but it makes the days better."

Another grunt.

"What if you know beforehand..." His hand flexed on the arm of the chair, the tattoo pumping once. "If you know you wouldn't make her days better, you'd make them worse."

"Not ideal."

"No," he said.

"What if she'd make your days better?"

"Bad arrangement for her."

"But what if?" I said.

"Man who took that deal would be selfish and wouldn't deserve her."

"Are you positive you'd make Noelle's days worse?"

He sniffed. A little smile.

"Who says I'm talking about me, *amigo*."

"Rocky claims he's no longer in the mafioso," I said.

"He's lying. I don't change and neither does he. *Hombre*'s a criminal." He finished the margarita in one long pull. Stood and took Kix from my lap. "Not going to their dumbass *gringo* wedding."

He stepped inside and walked up the stairs and I remained where I was, in case something in the universe needed fixing.

As long as it wasn't marriage that needed fixing.

Or the fallen nature of man.

Or myself.

Or anything else really.

I was halfway through the margarita and wondering if I'd get alcohol poisoning from it when a pickup truck braked in a slow squeal, one block east of my house. The headlights extinguished and I lost it in the dark and the leaves, but I heard four doors open and shut.

No voices though.

My phone buzzed. I pulled it from my pocket. An incoming call from Police Chief Jake Robertson.

How about that.

I sipped some fortifying tequila and answered the call.

"Chief. I hope you brought Whiteside with you," I said.

"Ahhh. How's that?" The words came through the phone and a split second later from the truck a block away.

"Whiteside and I need to convene. Walk him on down," I said.

"August, seems you already know this, but this's Jake Robertson and I was passing through Roanoke and wondered if you and I needed to have another chat about your involvement in the Caleb James debacle. The got'damn Caleb James debacle. From what I hear—"

"Whiteside. Is he with you? How many'd you bring?" I said.

"Ah," he said again. He was probably peering at my house, wondering how I'd spotted him so quickly. Unaware I'd been on the front porch fixing the universe.

"You came here to scare me. It worked. I'm so scared I might move to Bermuda. But Whiteside hit me in the back of the head when I wasn't ready and I am aggrieved."

"You're aggrieved."

"Reparations must be made."

"August, let's us go get a beer and talk about Caleb James," said Robertson.

I hung up. Set the phone down. Drank another swallow of margarita and descended the front steps to the concrete walk. The night was warm and humidity hung in the air like haze and I felt a looseness in my chest.

I shouted, "Whiteside."

There came some laughter from the pickup truck.

"You only approach a man when he isn't looking? Let's go," I said.

Four figures detached from the distant truck and walked toward me. They flared into relief under a streetlight and I saw short powerful bald Robertson and big thick Whiteside and two others.

"August, I got some stuff needs saying about Caleb James and Ervin Lane. Best said over a drink," said Robertson and they came on.

I wore a t-shirt and Levi jeans. Shorts would be better, but I'd already picked the fight.

Whiteside wore a light jacket over his t-shirt and he shrugged out of it.

They breached the perimeter of my lawn.

I pointed at the two men I didn't know.

"Either of you two see me fall down in the Lynchburg police department?"

One of the guys, fat around the middle and under his jaw, laughed. "Yeah I was there. I *saw you fall*."

"After Whiteside, consider yourself convoked," I said.

"Ain't nothing gonna happen after Whiteside," said Whiteside. He still had a great superhero jaw and was thick in the forearms and shoulders.

"What was the plan? Invade my house?" I said. "Shoot me in my sleep, kill my family?"

"Naw we just wanna talk, August," said Robertson.

"Need four guys to talk," I said.

"Told you, we were passing through."

"Talking's gonna have to wait. I'm too embarrassed to talk. Me and Whiteside gotta defend our honor," I said.

"Defend my honor." He laughed at how obtuse I was. "I got nothing to defend."

"Sure you do. You hit me in the back of the head. Makes you a coward. You gotta feel awful about being a coward. You're forced to beat me face-to-face to redeem yourself, else you'll remain a coward and not be able to sleep."

"Right here on your damn front lawn?" Whiteside was grinning.

"Look'it his face," said the other guy. "From where he fell down, he's busted up."

"Gently used, sir. I am gently used."

It was always awkward, two guys squaring up to fight each other. Who starts? That was one of the great things about official boxing matches—they had a bell. It rang to start the match and it rang to stop it. But me and Whiteside didn't have a bell. He didn't know how to begin, and it embarrassed him. And who would tell us when it was over?

"Right here, right now?" said Whiteside.

"What, you can only hit when my back's turned," I said.

He punched me.

Like all cops, Whiteside was trained in combat, some of it hand-to-hand. But he was one of the guys who got by on being bigger and stronger. He hit me the way a bully would, rearing back like about throwing a baseball, too long, too wild. He caught me on the shoulder because I twisted. It hurt and I felt an instant numbness below it.

I kicked him in the shin. They never anticipate the shin kick. It's short and quick and painful. He was throwing another punch but his shin hurt him and he kinda fell that way and he hopped, the punch grazing my shirt.

He said, "Fucker kicked my leg," and I turned into a left cross. I aimed for his nose, but he was staggering and I hit his mouth, stung my knuckles.

Hit him a right, missed again, dammit, hit him in the ear, a meaty thunk.

Just two idiots missing their targets over and over.

From his stagger he punched me in the ribs. A strong chop and it hurt. Anywhere but my nose. I hit him a left jab, connected with his nose, finally, then another, got him again, pop-pop, tried a big right but he got his arms up and grabbed my neck with both hands. His big thumbs squeezing at my aorta, my windpipe, closing anything he could. I couldn't breathe. I bought my hands down on his forearms, once, twice, no luck, no oxygen, a weird pain in my brain. Blood piling in a knot I felt above my shoulder. I kicked him between his legs. They don't see that coming either. He said, "Oh shit," but didn't let go so I did it again. His khakis were tight and I made solid contact.

One of his friends was going to hit me in the back of my head soon but I couldn't do anything about it.

The vice around my throat eased so I could breathe. He was in pain but I didn't care. I hit him the big right, his mouth again, putting my shoulder behind it, all my weight going forward, and he fell backward with it, his knees knocked together. I weighed around two hundred and twenty and he caught every pound. He landed unconscious, which I thought was good for him.

I coughed and my throat rattled.

Manny said, "Hey, *amigo*," and I turned in time to see the guy behind me pause. The guy behind me had been about to hit me in the head with a blackjack but Manny emerged from the shadows and said, "Hey, *amigo*," like a handsome Hispanic ghost, and the guy paused and now pivoted and took Manny's elbow to the teeth.

The guy fell and Manny dropped beside him, kneeling, and hit him again. And again. Looked like he was aiming for the man's eye.

"Hit *migo* in the back of his head, with a blackjack." Manny sounded mildly insane. Hit him again, a wet sound. "*Pedazo de mierda, vino a mi casa, pego a mi amigo en la cabeza, te mataré.*"

"Enough!" A flashlight clicked on. Robertson held it in

his left hand. In his right he held a revolver. "Jesus Christ, spic, you'll kill him. Who in the hell are you?"

I shook my right hand, the knuckles throbbing.

"Two down," I said. "Two more to go."

"I got the gun, August, and I'm fixing to arrest you for assaulting a police officer. They aren't even moving, got'-damn. We came here to talk."

"Bullshit to talk. You brought three guys with you."

Manny stood, His right hand was shining with dark blood from the guy's face. He looked at Robertson as a lion does a lamb.

Robertson saw the danger there, saw the wildfire in Manny's eyes. "Easy, guy. I got the gun."

"I can fit the whole gun in your ear, *policía*."

"I don't know who in the hell you are, but you're under arrest too. We came here to talk to August and you assaulted an officer of the law. God almighty. Normand, call 911. These boys still aren't moving. We need an ambulance, I reckon."

Normand, the last guy standing beside Robertson, took a phone from his pocket. His hands were shaking.

Manny hit Normand. One thunderous left, like Tyson, caught him flush in the cheek, and Normand dropped like the power'd gone out. He fell forward and Manny had to step out of the way. Normand's phone dropped into my grass.

"*Jesus*, enough! I swear to God!"

"It's over, Robertson," I said. "I know."

Robertson took two steps away from us, far enough so Manny couldn't reach him. "Get down, get down right fucking now or I'll shoot you both. I said right now!"

"You won't shoot."

"The hell I won't," he said.

"You have no good reason for being here, Robertson. I'm

investigating your department for corruption, and you being here makes you look guilty as hell. Put away your revolver before this federal marshal makes you eat it."

"Corruption? I'll tell you what's corrupt, you hitting these three boys who did nothing wrong," he said. "You said federal marshal? Ain't no way."

"I know everything, Robertson. I know Caleb didn't fire the gun. I know Ervin did and you doctored the tape to add a second gunshot. I know it and I can prove it."

"You..." Robertson's eyes had gone even wider. Poor man looked like he needed to sit down but he thought Manny might bite him. "I don't know what in the hell you're talking about."

"Yeah you do." I shook my hand again. "Don't be stupid. Why else would you be here?"

"I... No, we figure that out later. Get on the ground. I'm giving you to three and then I shoot. You hear? *One.*" His gun was pointed at me. Kinda. He didn't look happy about it. A man who thought he'd be okay swimming with sharks as long as no sharks showed up but they did.

"Don't do it, Robertson. You already lost. Have the good sense to admit it."

"*Two.*" He barked the word.

Manny drew his Glock from the holster at the small of his back and moved sideways away from me, like the second hand of a clock moving in reverse. Getting behind Robertson, aiming at his ear.

"You fire, I fire, *amigo.*"

"No," said Robertson. "No no." Now he didn't know where to aim. "You're a marshal, aren't you? Well by god help me arrest this man."

"Don't think we're gonna do that. Put the revolver away."

Some of the ambient light caught Robertson's bald head. He was sweating and blue veins were visible above his ears.

"Chief Robertson." Manny spoke soft and it was scary.

"What in the *hell* are you doing? Get that gun off me! I'm a cop, for God's sake!"

"Time's up."

"*Okay!*" Robertson let go and the pistol fell into the dirt and he shined his flashlight on it. "Okay, there, okay? I'll be the bigger man here. Now let me make a phone call and we'll sort this out, and maybe you won't lose your job, you understand that?"

"No phone calls," I said. "Just us."

"August." Robertson held his hands out to me, like—*see reason, you idiot*. "You're a private cop. You know the life. You know how got'damn hard it is. Ervin, he was... Dammit, the man was doing his best. I wanted to help a fellow officer, is all."

Manny hit him too. The same hard left. Manny punched like a jackhammer and, like Normand, Robertson fell hard. Lights out, backward instead of forward, one boot rising up as he did, the other planted in the ground. His head thunked on my concrete walkway.

And then there were none.

"You're awfully mean," I said.

"*Mierda.*" Manny shook the left hand. "Think I cracked a bone. *Uy, eso duele.*"

"Maybe if you quit hitting people. They caught you on the wrong night, all broken-hearted and mad."

"Don't be an ass, *señor*," said Manny. "I don't have a heart."

I felt shaky and my stomach was tight. Relieved none of the guns were fired.

"You only got one." He pointed to the bodies on the lawn. "I got three."

"Who's counting."

"Me. Three-to-one."

"You're being glib for a guy who decked a police chief."

Manny holstered the Glock and shook out his right hand, both hands now. I was doing it with my right hand and we looked ludicrous.

"Glib isn't a word. But..." He squinted at the ground. "This was a helluva tourist."

"A tourist," I said.

"*Sí.* You didn't tell me this tourist was coming."

"Mmmm," I said.

"Tourist. Like trouble. You said it the other day. Stupid gringo word."

I nodded. "Tsuris."

"What I said. Tourist."

Inside my house, GPA was barking. Lights snapped on. Stackhouse came out.

"What in the hell," she said.

My gut was still constricted with the fight and violence. "Manny punched a police chief."

"Rusty Hastings?"

"Different chief. Lynchburg," I said.

"Guy was about to shoot Mack. I should've let him, *sí*?"

"Is he out?" said Stackhouse.

"You think I miss? I don't miss."

"Why are you two idiots smiling about it?" She walked down the steps.

"Margaritas."

"Only one but it felt like four," I said.

Whiteside groaned on the ground. One of the other guys tried to sit up.

"All over our lawn like litter. What the hell are they doing here?" Stackhouse wore pajamas and carried her cell.

"Getting their ass kicked," said Manny.

I closed my eyes and winced. "Rats."

"What?"

"This means I gotta arrest Ervin Lane tomorrow. Before he hears the game's up and takes off," I said.

Ronnie and Timothy came outside too. Timothy held GPA by a leash. She strained and whined.

GPA, not Ronnie.

Ronnie said, "It appears as though someone might need a good lawyer."

"I bet," Timothy said with a sigh, "our neighbors wish we'd move."

# 30

I collected the cell phones of Robertson, Whiteside, and the other two. Between me, Stackhouse, and Manny we had enough handcuffs and flex cuffs to restrain the four men. We didn't know what the hell to do with them yet, so we marched them into our basement, a dry concrete place we used for storage.

If we arrested them, poop would hit the fan. And I wasn't ready for that mess yet. We provided pillows and blankets and explained if they behaved for a few hours then maybe Manny wouldn't shoot them. One of the guys called his wife, told her he'd be working late. I held the phone.

We told them to sleep tight and we'd deal with it in the morning. Robertson told me to have a heart, that Ervin had made a mistake, that no one should be crucified for it, to put myself in his shoes, that if I didn't let him out soon I'd be hanged, which I thought improbable. I locked the door to the basement and opened my laptop to book two airline tickets.

~

Manny and I caught a preposterously early flight out of Roanoke. A small jet with a single stewardess who pulled down her mask when serving us so Manny could see she was pretty. It was a short hop to Atlanta, then a two-hour layover during which we drank coffee and ate Cinnabon. I questioned the carbs and Manny told me to shut it and asked if I'd ever seen Scarface because if Noelle married Rocky then she would die like Gina did in that movie.

We boarded a larger plane with *two* stewardesses and lifted off for Evansville, Indiana. I caught a nap and Manny read about capitalism and investments. When I woke he told me that Marxists were going to ruin everything and they should be shipped to Australia. A stewardess brought me a mimosa, because she knew I was *society*, and I told Manny not to ruin my flight with his propaganda.

"You were hired to find Caleb James, *sí*?"

"Correct," I said.

"You still don't know where he is."

"I don't. But if we prove that he's innocent, which he is, his father can get him a message. Or Robin can," I said.

"And he'll come back, a free man."

"Presumably. And me, the victor."

"Who is Robin?" said Manny.

The stewardess brought Manny another cup of ice, which he used to ice his purple left hand. She made a pouty face, her mask down, and touched Manny on the shoulder and said, "Poor baby," and she reluctantly moved on to tend mere mortals.

"I am not a baby. Who is Robin?"

"A girl who dated both Ervin and Caleb. She's a mom now, I'm positive, I'm nearly positive, and the child belongs to one of those two men. I think. She knows where Caleb is," I said.

"In Mexico?"

"Could be he's in Mexico. It doesn't matter where, if I convince him to return of his own accord," I said.

"We gonna ruin Ervin's life this morning. So you can finish your job."

"Maybe."

"Maybe? Ay, why are we on this plane, in *coach*, if it's maybe?" said Manny.

"I haven't figured out what I'm gonna do yet."

"Should hurry. We land in a few minutes, kemosabe."

"You're ruining my mimosa. Haven't you noticed I'm *society*?" I said.

"You're society with a swollen hand and busted nose."

"I don't know if you're allowed to say kemosabe. It's Native American appropriation."

"I can. You can't. I looked it up. Weird woke penalties only apply to White people," said Manny.

"That doesn't seem fair."

"Those are the rules. I didn't make them up."

"Who did?" I said.

"Angry White *señoritas* in college. I read it in an article."

I nodded thoughtfully. "They do seem to have a lot of power."

"Maybe they don't know what they're saying, but *señoritas* are loud about it."

"Gotta be loud about something. I pick the Washington Nationals," I said.

We landed at the regional airport and I rented a Chevy Cruze, certainly the same car as my previous visit, and Manny drove it because he wanted to go faster. The whole way he swooned over the fertile countryside and the landscape of opportunities and freedom and Uncle Sam and the

Declaration of Independence and the cotton gin and bourbon.

After an hour of it, though, he was bored and wanted to see a city with people in it.

Washington, Indiana remained a quiet, self-contained city. We motored through and the residents watched us as placid as the cows. Manny remarked it looked like the town in that Mayberry show with Andy Griffith. West on Cosby, south on Akester, into the infinite countryside again, and we parked off the road a quarter-mile from Ervin Lane's home, which we couldn't see over corn that was already being harvested in nearby fields.

We listened to the engine click, and some cows mooed, and in the distance a big combine was droning quietly.

"I like this guy," I said. "I don't want to spook him. I'll go in and we talk and figure it out."

Manny handed me his service Glock. The airline let him carry his but didn't let me carry mine. Which was, I thought, hurtful.

"*Buena suerte,*" he said.

"He needs to be punched in the face, I'll call you."

Manny's knuckles were red and swollen.

"Ay, I can give him a mean right. Only once," he said. "Also freedom smells like cow poop."

I left him in the Cruze and walked stiffly down the endless road to Ervin's doublewide trailer.

No truck. Ervin wasn't home.

How anticlimactic. I checked my watch. Noon local time. Maybe he was out to lunch.

I walked his empty driveway, crunching on gravel, to his backyard. The farm-life accoutrement fascinated me. Farmers did what they could, the best they could, with what they had. Ervin collected rainwater in buckets from his gutters, probably to water the pigs. He kept a rotating barrel where his food scraps composted with chicken poop to create 'black gold.' The chickens roamed behind a wire fence patched with twine. Looked like he'd recently replaced the roof of the coop, and he kept the old corrugated metal because he'd find some use for it. He'd mowed the grass and raked the clippings into a pile to use as fertilizer, maybe?

Nothing wasted, everything given a second purpose, a new life.

The pigs were in a wooden enclosure beyond the chickens. These didn't look like great hogs; they were small and pink. They swarmed over one another toward me, in case I brought food. Corn grains dotted the ground outside the sty, where they'd fallen. The pigs probably fed on corn that Ervin'd grown himself.

I was staring from the pigpen toward the house, thinking about the little pink heart visible in the window, when Manny called. "Truck approaching. Could be Farmer Ervin."

It was. Ervin's big Ford F-150 pulled into the drive and I ducked out of view behind the one-story barn. I felt ludicrous hiding but last time I'd been here he told me not to come back and he'd worn a pistol on his belt and I was tired of angry guys pointing a gun at me.

Behind the barn he kept rusted shovels and rakes. A short stack of buckets. Unopened packets of mouse traps. A bag of snake repellant. Some animal had been digging a hole near the far corner, a mound of fresh black earth.

If I saw a snake, I would open fire immediately.

A truck door opened and closed. Then another, and the truck bed slammed. Would he come out to the barn? Shocking a man with PTSD out here wouldn't be ideal.

Mackenzie August, caught with his hand in the cookie jar.

I examined the fresh hole an animal had been digging. Groundhog? Fox? Fox trying to get a groundhog? Wolf? Mole? Long as it wasn't a snake.

"Hey."

It was Ervin calling out. His voice startled me, sudden and loud. By the sound, he stood near the trailer.

I didn't respond.

I crouched by the hole to get a better look at it. It was maybe two feet deep. On my knees, I scooped loose dirt out. The animal had been trying to get at something. I scooped more. The animal had been successful. Eating the flesh off an old bone.

"*Hey.* I got a call. About trespassers. I don't know who you are, but I know you're back here. Come on out," said Ervin. "Quit snooping around."

I scooped and I scooped.

And I stopped and I held my breath and my heart thudded.

Because I was looking at the remains of a human foot.

PART of my brain working independently coalesced facts into possible storylines.

-Ervin moved out here, still a drunk. Killed a neighbor. Buried him. The shock of it forced him to attend AA.

-Ervin killed Robin Lucas. Jealous rage because she'd left him for Caleb. Buried her in his backyard, right after she and I talked on the phone.

-Caleb, fresh out of prison, found Ervin in Indiana and

tried to kill him, failed, and he was buried here. That's why I couldn't find him.

-Ervin dated a local girl, the girl who gave him the pink heart. Got drunk. Killed her. Buried her.

-Ervin killed...

It didn't matter who. Not right now.

Ervin had killed and buried a person.

He was a killer.

He and I wouldn't be able to talk this out.

I TRIED NOT TO VOMIT.

The decomposing toes were partially eaten. Purple and green.

I rose to my feet and stepped away from the hole in the ground. My face was pale, I knew it, I felt it.

I came around the barn and Ervin did a jump. He hadn't known if I was hiding in the corn stalks, or the shed, or the barn, or wherever. I held Manny's pistol pointed at the ground. A Glock 27, too small for my big hand.

I wanted to say something hilarious but I might throw up if I did.

"I recognize you," said Ervin.

Ervin's appearance was a surprise again. No longer the swollen fat cop. I'd forgotten how healthy he looked; the shaved head and black tattoos looked out of place. He'd lost a lot of fat and muscle to sobriety and a healthier diet. His left arm ended at the heavy prosthesis, thick fingers good for holding a bucket or rake.

But he'd killed and buried someone behind his barn.

"You're the private cop out of Roanoke. Last time you

came out, we sat and had a lemonade. Now you're carrying a gun," he said.

"Sorry about this, Ervin."

"Sorry about what?"

"You need to sit on the ground," I said.

"I asked you to leave this alone. I asked you politely, man-to-man."

"I didn't."

"I see that," said Ervin.

"Sit down on the ground."

"Tell me what you think you know," he said.

"I know everything."

"You *think* you know everything."

"Sit on the ground." We weren't close enough for him to attack me. I wasn't in danger. But I wasn't thinking clearly either. Still in some shock.

"And then what?"

"You're under arrest, Ervin."

That startled him. He peered at me and shook his head.

"You think you know. But you don't. It would've been better for both of us if you left it alone," he said.

"What don't I know?"

"There's a whole world of things you don't know."

"Ervin. In a few more seconds I'll fire a warning shot over your head. That'll alert my partner to join us. If I fire again after that, it'll be at you. And I don't want to do that. Sit down."

"No."

"Yes," I said.

"I'm not going back." He turned on his heel and marched toward the doublewide. Daring me to shoot him. But I wasn't a guy who shot other guys in the back.

"Ervin," I shouted. "Ervin, stop."

He didn't. He opened the rear screen door and disappeared inside. Gone.

"Dammit," I said.

He was gonna get a rifle and open a window and take aim.

I was thirty yards from the house. A tough shot, especially through a window, unless he had a scope. He'd miss, but even still, I hated being shot at so much. The retort would burst his eardrums inside the room and I'd have to move quick.

But no. The door opened again and Ervin marched back. He carried a shotgun.

I raised my pistol. Cradled it with two hands. Weaver stance, aiming at a spot in the earth between us.

"Ervin, you aim that thing at me, I have no choice."

He was smiling. A sad smile.

He was crying.

"I knew this day would come, you know. I knew someone would show up here. I practiced it in my mind. Walked through what I'd do. And here we are." He blinked at the moisture in his eyes.

Inside the house, a new sound.

A woman crying.

My heart sank, a depression building in my chest.

"Who's in the house, Ervin?"

"I'm not going back." He shook his head, tears winking on his cheeks. "I decided that early on. I'd die first. I *will* die first. But I also decided I'd give the man who came to get me a chance. A chance to leave and let me run. Because I'd try to kill him and if that didn't work I'd kill myself. That is, unless he let me run."

"Put the shotgun down. Don't aim it at me. Who's inside your home?" I said.

The barrel of his shotgun was aimed near my feet. It was a lightweight Remington, a pump twelve-gauge with a pistol grip. He held the grip with his right hand. The fingers of his plastic left hand were kinda wrapped around the slide. I didn't know if he could jack another round with the prosthesis or not.

"What do you say? Are you letting me go? Or are we shooting this out. I'm ready," he said.

"I'm not doing either of those. Put that down."

"I explained this to you. I'm not going back."

"Not going back *where*?" I said.

He raised the barrel of his shotgun a few inches. An alarm between my ears. Tension in my arms. I raised my own barrel too. We were twenty-five yards apart. His shotgun wouldn't kill me at this distance. Wouldn't feel good. It'd put me in the hospital, and a surgeon would have to dig shot out of my chest and stomach. But also it wouldn't create a baseball sized hole through me.

I hated being shot at.

The woman inside grew louder. She was shouting, *No, no, don't! Please!* She was visible at the window, above the pink heart.

"Stay inside!" I shouted at her.

"Put the gun down or I shoot," he said.

"No!" shouted the woman. "*Caleb, no!*"

My heart lurched.

"Times up," he said.

He raised the shotgun.

The world tilted.

A little kid inside started to cry too. A little kid at the door. The woman grabbed him away, still shouting at us both.

I couldn't see straight. Couldn't focus.

I lowered my gun.

"Wait," I said.

"I can't wait. We're both out of time."

"Wait." I dropped the Glock. I stepped away from it, trying to make the world stop spinning. "Wait. Did she call you Caleb?"

## 31

A lightning strike between my ears. A burst of brilliance, flashing on dark secrets.

I was no longer looking at Ervin Lane, drunken cop who'd lost a lot of weight.

I was looking at Caleb James, a fugitive who'd shaved his head, and tattooed his arms, and grown a goatee. He was him. He was... They were swapped. They were each other. They...

Vertigo. My altered understanding of reality. As if I looked at my reflection to find it acting on its own accord. I was sitting in Ervin's grass. In Caleb's grass.

"You're not Ervin Lane," I heard myself say.

The man with the shotgun lowered the barrel so it no longer pointed at me. In a better state of mind, I'd appreciate the gesture.

"You're Caleb James. You're Caleb James, but you shaved your head and grew a goatee and put on weight."

"Putting on weight was the hardest part," said the man with the shotgun.

"That means..." I jerked a thumb over my shoulder.

"The guy buried behind your shed is... I don't know anything."

Caleb James, fugitive on the run, twisted at the waist to speak over his shoulder.

"Robin. Come bring this man some water? Before he passes out? He dropped his gun."

Inside the trailer, the kid kept crying and he called for his father.

～

THE FOUR OF us sat at the kitchen table. Me, Manny, Caleb James, and Robin Lucas. A cheap particle board table with vinyl surface. The living room floor was decorated with toy cars. The refrigerator with color scribbles held on by magnets.

Manny was bouncing the boy on his knees and the boy was saying, "UhhhhUhhhUhhhUhhh," with each bounce and smiling at the sound.

The Remington shotgun was propped in the corner. Caleb decided he didn't need it, and it would do him no good if he did.

We both had some explaining to do, and my wits had returned to earth.

"You were here to arrest Ervin Lane," said Robin. "Why?"

I told them. About my investigation. My run-in with Lynchburg police and the doctored video. That I knew Caleb was innocent of Kim Harper's death, that I could prove it, and they both started crying. Then I pointed out that although he was innocent of Kim's death, he had killed Ervin Lane. Or Robin had, one of the two, I didn't know yet, so don't start celebrating.

That sobered the mood.

"I'm still hazy on some details, so let me reconstruct the order of events." I sipped lemonade. "And you tell me what I get wrong."

Caleb nodded without speaking. Robin looked at him and then at me, and the kid laughed.

"Caleb, two years ago, you're in jail, awaiting trial. You don't remember what happened the night of the arrest, but you can't believe you would grab a cop's gun and shoot him, especially not a guy you've known your whole life. It makes no sense, but they have a video that incriminates you, and the story to back it up. To make it worse, while in jail, Robin tells you she's pregnant."

Robin was still significantly pretty. She looked out of place in the trailer, next to a man with a bad goatee and a shaved head and black tattoos on his neck.

"I left Ervin a few weeks earlier. I left him for Caleb and we, well, we picked up where we left off. If that makes sense, Mr. August," she said.

"So you were pregnant. But you were unsure which man was the father."

"And *so* worried the world would find out."

"But you did tell Caleb," I said.

"Do you know what those bastards did?" said Caleb. "They slipped me crystal meth. I'd been drying out for over a week, and one of the cops tossed me a baggie and left the door open. I'm ashamed of this, I am, but I was depressed and crying. I knew I'd be in jail my whole life and I'd found out Robin was pregnant, and the deputy sheriff tosses me a baggie of meth. What was I supposed to do?"

"Eat the meth," said Manny.

Caleb nodded. "I did. Like a starving man."

"And the cop left the jail door open," I said.

"It's ludicrous. But yes."

"That's where the video of you attacking guards comes from," I said. "You were high and on a mission to get the hell out of there."

"Yes. Again, I'm not proud of it. But they baited me. I wasn't backing down from my innocence and they needed more ammunition."

"They used that video, and the video of the botched arrest, to coerce you into a plea deal. And the deal felt dirty to you, but it was too good to pass up," I said.

"That's precisely it. I know good terms when I see them."

"They send you to Wallens Ridge, and Robin moves away from Lynchburg."

Robin kept nodding. "I felt like Hester Prynne. I couldn't live there anymore."

"So Caleb is in prison," I said, "and feeling worse and worse about the plea deal, and he wants to raise his own son, and he concocts a plan to break out."

Caleb reached across the table with his one good hand to take the little boy's fingers.

"The wildest part?" Caleb smiled. "My son Simon. Look at him. Does he look like me?"

"He looks more like Ervin," I said.

"He's Ervin's son. Not mine. The wildest part is, I didn't care. I would raise any child of Robin's. I refused to remain incarcerated. Or, I refused not to try."

Manny nodded his approval.

I rejoined. "You and the librarian hit it off. He's quitting the prison soon and agrees to smuggle you in the trunk of his car. He thinks you're innocent and he hates the place, and the plan goes smoothly. You return to Lynchburg to collect some money from your father's safe deposit box. Good so far?"

Caleb looked out the window for a long time. Looked at the pink valentine and the corn beyond.

He said, "I will neither confirm nor deny the involvement of the librarian and my father."

"Something I don't understand. Why set Ervin's house on fire?" I said.

Robin gave a dark laugh. "Oh no. Ervin did that himself."

"Did he."

"Ervin threatened to sue me if I didn't let him see his son occasionally. He knew a court would never give him parental rights, and I didn't want the drama, so we compromised. I visited and brought Simon every few months. Ervin never cared, though. He was always stone cold drunk. I was there that day, Mr. August. I'm the one who told Ervin that Caleb escaped prison. We were standing in the garage and his hands were shaking and he was trying to light a cigarette. I told him about Caleb and he dropped his Zippo lighter. He said he was going to kill me and I ran with Simon and he chased us. Next thing we knew, his garage was up in flames. I drove off. And of course he and his cop buddies spun the story to implicate Caleb," said Robin. "Redneck bastards."

"Meanwhile, Caleb tells Marky he'll pay for rehab and then he vanishes into the blue. For months."

Caleb grinned. "I lived in a tent at a Jellystone park in Kentucky. Nice weather for it. Enjoying my freedom. Making plans with Robin. Until she stopped returning my calls."

Robin gave another dark laugh, like a woman who'd come to expect only awful things.

"Ervin shows up at my door. By then he'd already retired and moved out here, but he drives all the way to my apartment, Mr. August. He beats me, ties me up, tosses me into the back seat of his truck, and drives the whole night, a miracle we didn't crash, bringing me and Simon here. He's drunk and drinking constantly, stopping to pee on the side of the road, telling me we're starting a new family. We reach his trailer and he doesn't untie me. He locks me in the spare bedroom and keeps me there for *eight* days. Eight days, listening to Simon cry. It was hell on earth. Hell in a doublewide. Ervin kept threatening to kill him if I didn't cooperate, or if I tried to run away. He would drink himself unconscious and Simon would crawl to my door and try to open it but we couldn't, both of us crying."

"But." Caleb raised a finger. "He'd brought her phone with her. A burner phone, and we'd shared our location with each other. After a few days of no calls or texts, I followed the phone to its last known location. Here."

"And you killed Ervin."

"I feel no shame about this part. Ervin was standing at the pigpen, urinating on them. It's true, I saw it with my own eyes, peeing on the pigs and laughing. This whole farm was falling apart. I crept into the trailer, found Robin locked in the spare bedroom. Simon staring blankly at the television. Of course he didn't know who I was. I couldn't open the spare bedroom door, but I spotted his Remington shotgun in the master, a round in the chamber. I took it, walked outside, and killed him."

"One shot?" said Manny.

"First time I'd ever fired a weapon. I got close. One shot. Didn't say a word to him, and I sat there until I knew he was dead. Made damn sure of it. I have no nightmares, no regrets," said Caleb and he spoke the words like hammering the armor on again. "But here's the part that amazes us both. Ervin is still lying dead at the pigpen, and I haven't figured out how to unlock Robin, when someone knocks on the door. I peer through the window, and it's a police officer. I tell Robin I have to run, that she's safe now, and we'll be together soon. But there's another officer at the back door. I can't flee. I'm busted. I walk outside, ready to be arrested, and you know what happens? The police officer smiles at me. He says, 'Good afternoon, Mr. Lane, sorry to bother you. We received a call from Chief Robertson, asking us to check on you as a favor to him. He says you're an old friend not returning his messages and he's worried about you.'"

The boy, bored and restless, squirmed away from Manny and wobbled into the living room to play with cars.

"Cops didn't know what you were supposed to look like," said Manny.

"That's right." Caleb was grinning. "They both assumed I was Ervin. They said, 'You look like you're doing okay,' and I said, 'I am, thank you, my phone's broken but I'll get it fixed and call Chief Robertson,' and they left. They never saw Ervin lying near the pigs. I broke Robin's door down and we were reunited."

"And you buried Ervin behind the shed. Poorly."

"My first time burying a body. I didn't dig deep enough. Animals have been back there half a dozen times," he said. "It's disgusting."

"Are you going to turn us in?" Robin was focused on the next awful thing she expected to happen to her.

"Keep going with the story," I said.

"We stayed here for that weekend, deciding what to do. Where do we run? Mexico? Canada? And a check came in the mail on Monday. Ervin was drawing disability. And I told Robin, as long as we remain in this trailer, the checks will keep coming. And wouldn't that be something."

"Can't be much," I said.

"No, but I'm a wanted man. It's more than I can make, obviously. Robin said Ervin had no friends here. He lived alone, didn't talk to anyone at the grocery store. It wouldn't take much to fool the locals. If I shaved my head and grew a goatee..." Caleb shrugged.

"You duped me. Us talking and drinking lemonade out back, me the biggest idiot in the world, talking to the man I was hunting," I said.

"I got away with it because you'd never met the real Ervin."

"Still," said Manny. "Humiliating for Mack. So embarrassing."

It was, in fact.

I pointed at Caleb's neck. "You even have the tattoos."

He did another shrug. "I always wanted some. It took few weeks to ink the visible ones. A guy forty-five minutes north of here, and he never asked questions. He went off photographs online."

"And you started pounding cheeseburgers," I said.

"I drink weight-gainer shakes."

"And occasionally you visit Skip James, who has a playhouse for Simon out back that he didn't want me to find, but I did."

"Wow." Robin's eyes widened. "You're thorough."

"And then," I said, "you chopped off your arm."

Caleb laughed and waggled the prosthesis.

"Looks good doesn't it." He ran his finger underneath the forearm, up to the hand. A seam I hadn't noticed parted, and he worked to wiggle the blocky thing loose. No wonder I'd always thought it looked big and heavy—his entire hand was inside. A grisly magic trick, pulling one hand off to reveal another. His real hand looked shriveled and pale, like limbs look coming out of a cast. He flexed his withered fingers, wincing with the pain. "They get stiff in there."

"*Ay dios*," said Manny.

Caleb thunked the prosthetic hand on the table. The fingers didn't budge. "To be more realistic, it's a hard prosthesis. I can't move them."

"You wear that thing all day."

"All day, even working out back in case..." He nodded at me. "In case I get visitors." He stood and rinsed his arm in the sink, and washed out the plastic, because it smelled like sweat. "You wouldn't believe the options online, for ordering prosthetic hands."

"This is preposterous."

"Maybe. But it's my best shot." Caleb shrugged again. He liked doing that. "We had a scare when the lady from social services came by. She does quarterly checks, and she'd met Ervin once before. We chatted for thirty minutes about my lifestyle, and the only thing she said about my appearance was that I looked healthier. We knew we'd done a convincing job then."

"You really attend Alcoholic Anonymous," I said.

"You bet. It helps. Somewhere inside me is a man who still craves shit he shouldn't have. It's not alcohol, but it's something."

"Mr. August, you told me on the phone that you were the only man who wanted to help Caleb," said Robin. She was leaning across the table toward me, her brows knotted upward. "Now you know he's truly innocent, and he's out here doing his best. His absolute best. He's *happy*. We're happy."

"It's true, I am. To be honest, Mr. August, I don't even mind the fake hand. I was high on meth that night. I'm at least partially responsible for Kim Harper's death. It's my penance. I'm not dodging my culpability in this," he said.

"What's your long-term plan?" I said.

"Save enough money to move. Probably to Mexico. I like it here a lot. This lifestyle suits us both. We're a little happy family. Simon likes feeding the chickens. But we know this is temporary. Sooner or later the world will catch up, and we need to be gone by then. I texted everyone in Ervin's phone, and asked for twelve months of privacy, so hopefully..." He raised his hands, palm up. "Hopefully we have six more months."

I finished my lemonade. I stood and set the glass in the sink. Looked out the window. Looked at the heart Robin had made for Caleb. Looked at their little piece of earth. A small farm spoiling under Ervin, now orderly, and profitable and happy. I walked to the corner and picked up the Remington and felt the young couple tense. I racked the slide five times to eject three shells.

"Where's your pistol?"

"Where's my pistol," he repeated.

"You have a pistol. Tell me where."

He swallowed.

"Above the microwave. In the cabinet," he said.

I found it. The pistol he'd worn under his shirt last time I was here. A Glock 19. Probably Ervin's service piece.

"No more guns in the house?"

"No sir," said Caleb. "He only had those, and I can't buy one."

I walked through the screen door, onto the back patio. Manny followed. He wore his own Glock, smaller than Ervin's, in his holster. We walked to the chickens, hideous things without intelligence making low bobbling noises.

Above us the azure never ended.

"Let's grill a pig," said Manny.

"I don't know how."

"Shoot one in the head and put it over some fire and eat bacon."

"What about the skin?"

"Cut it off," said Manny.

"You and I would make terrible farmers."

"What about cops. We good at that?"

I turned to peer at the doublewide trailer.

"Still to be determined."

"Even if he didn't kill Harper, they can't go back to Lynchburg," said Manny.

"No. They'd be stained with it. He'd be at odds with the entire Court Street. And he's broken too many laws. He escaped from prison, impersonated a cop, falsified his identity, wrongfully cashed government checks."

"Killed Ervin."

"I don't mind that part," I said. "But Mother Justice might."

I stared at the animals a few minutes, like they had answers, and we walked back to their home and sat in the Adirondack chair on the rear patio. Inside, the television was making noise and so was Simon. The adults were quiet. Manny was too, and it gave me time to think. Think about guilt and innocence, and the work of growing up, and second chances and justice and duty and weeping Skip James and his little playhouse and Kim Harper and Samantha Miller and her Sunday School class calling for Caleb's head because he was Presbyterian and my role in it all.

"Kinda funny, *amigaso*. Both Ervin and Caleb kept telling you to leave the other one alone. Except both were Caleb," Manny said.

"Yeah."

"He played you, and you didn't pick up on it."

"He's convincing," I said. "Like Sarah Underwood told us, he's sharp."

"But you found him."

"Meh."

"Now all you gotta do is, take him in."

"I wish you'd quit bringing that up."

Manny grinned. "I like it when you don't know what to do. Makes this humble Puerto Rican feel better about himself."

"I know what I want to do," I said. "I just don't know how."

"While you're thinking," said Manny, "I'll pick us a pig to slaughter."

## 32

Late that night, Sheriff Stackhouse unlocked the door leading to our basement. The door swung wide, revealing four men below, staring upward, their faces swollen in various spots from their fight with me and Manny. Four men kept hostage for twenty-four hours.

Stackhouse held a riot gun taken from her trunk.

She said, "Move backward. Face the wall and touch your noses to it."

"Sheriff. Come on, now, this here won't do. You've *got* to let us out. How long have we known each other?" said Robertson.

"*Now,*" she said, and the men obeyed. She walked down the steps, followed by Manny, then me. Manny and I held pistols, in case. The riot gun wasn't loaded, so we wouldn't go deaf. Ronnie followed last. The basement looked yellow from the naked overhead bulbs, stark shadows where we blocked the light. Piles of blankets where they'd passed the time. "Robertson. You and your jackasses are in deep water. We know what you did. We know you framed an innocent man, we have proof of it, and you'll be lucky if you don't spend hard time. Defense attorney Ronnie Summers is behind me and she believes your best offer will be five years, more likely ten."

"Sheriff. Don't do this. We were trying to help a fellow cop, got'damn it. The boy made a mistake, is all," said Robertson.

Stackhouse took two steps forward and used the riot gun like a bat. She cracked Robertson above the ear and he staggered to his left and he cursed but didn't fall and she said, "You talk out of line again, Jake, and next time I won't miss your ear." Robertson's skin opened and blood welled. "You have one way through this that doesn't involve prison. If you're smart, you'll keep quiet and listen."

Stackhouse nodded at me over her shoulder. My cue.

I said, "Deputy Marshal Martinez and I flew to Indiana. To arrest Ervin. We all know he was drunk and accidentally killed Harper. He's guilty of murder. Caleb James isn't." I paused and Robertson said a really bad word under his breath. It stank down here. "We had a long talk. Me and Ervin. And the truth is, I couldn't do it. Ervin is thriving. He's doing great. He's off alcohol and working his little farm, and wants to be left alone. Even though he's the one who shot Kim, we flew home without him. Seems to me Ervin has paid enough. He's still there and wants you to leave him be for a full year. Maybe he'll return then. You follow all this so far?"

Tension had drained out from the four men. Two of them sagged against the wall.

"Yes, I follow you, August," said Robertson. "I'm obliged for it. Ervin, well, he wasn't like a son to me, but close to it."

"So we'll leave Ervin out there all alone. But in order to make this work, Robertson," I said, "you and I need to come to a new deal. And I set the terms."

## 33

Monday morning.

Georgina Princess, Kix, and I drove to the dog park near Lynchburg College, a mile from Court Street. Kix was skipping school for the event and he was worried his grades would suffer.

We unloaded in the parking lot and walked through the fence, and I unleashed the hound. Georgina Princess understood this was a place to run wild and she did, tearing away from the dirt patch near the gate and frolicking into the verdancy beyond. She had shade trees and a doggie water fountain to investigate, as well as a Cocker Spaniel, a brown Labrador, and a Golden Retriever to harass. Kix thought this a riot and trailed her, and every few minutes Georgina Princess would do a fly-by, Maverick style, and knock him clean off his feet.

Samantha Miller joined me fifteen minutes later. Although she claimed to adore GPA, she declined to enter the dog park. In her defense, there was mud and dog poo, and fur floated in the breeze, and I bet her shoes cost five hundred dollars. We met at the fence, me dirty, her clean and brilliant, Kix a disaster.

"On the way over, Mr. August, I listened to a news report on WFIR. Police Chief Jake Robertson claims Caleb James was spotted in France last week," said Samantha. She wore white linen pants and a gold loop belt and a bright pink tunic and her hair was tied up in a pony tail near the top of her head. "That must be the bad report you said you have for me?"

I nodded at her.

"Essentially."

"What had you planned on telling me, if I hadn't heard the report?" she said.

"That no matter how hard I looked, I would never be able to bring Caleb in. And I won't find him in Europe either."

She set her hands on the green fence and watched the dogs. She'd told me she had a teacup Yorkie, which was a small enough breed to sink entirely into some of the mud pits.

"So you failed," she said.

"Could put it that way."

"I was told, 'Don't work with a private detective!' I was told, 'They never do what they say they'll do,' and, 'You'll be sorry!' This is embarrassing for both of us." Samantha said it with enough bitterness to curdle my coffee.

"I put in more hours than you paid me for. So there's that."

"Are you *really* asking for more money?"

"I'm trying to justify not bringing Caleb's head to you on a platter. In fact..." I handed her a check.

"What is this?"

"A partial refund," I said.

She held the check by the corner like it was muddy.

"Why?" she said.

"Because the whole thing was rotten."

"How so?"

"Because Kim Harper is still dead. And no one was really innocent in this." Not even me. "And I wish the person responsible for her death was spending time in prison."

"Because you didn't catch him," she said. "And you feel guilty."

I made a shrug.

"Tell me the truth, Mr. August. Did you do your best? You failed, and it cost our class a large sum of money, even with this rebate, but... you tried, at least?"

"I did the best with what I had. I'm not happy, but I wouldn't change anything. Living on the run won't be easy for Caleb. He's still paying for his sins, even if you don't have the satisfaction of watching."

"Well." She folded the check and slipped it into a pocket. "Well," she said again and she bounced her hand on the fence, her rings clanging brightly on the metal. The rich girl born to privilege wasn't used to not getting what she wanted. "I suppose God works in mysterious ways."

"Sometimes the wicked go free and the innocent are punished, and sometimes it's the other way around, and we have to put our head down and work and trust."

"Even though it was decent of you to return some of the money, I'm afraid I can't give you a good reference, Mr. August, should anyone ask."

As I watched, Georgina Princess paused at the doggie water fountain, a metal bowl that refilled itself, and she drank and made a terrific mess.

"One of the hazards of my job. Dissatisfied clients."

"It's a shame, because I'd heard you were *so good*. I had such high hopes, such faith," she said.

"You'll find some other way to stick it to the Presbyterians."

"I suppose I will." She blinked and shook her head and took her hands off the fence like it'd electrocuted her. "No, that's not what I meant. It's not about the Presbyterians. Though to be honest they don't seem nearly penitent enough about the mess they created."

"Goodbye, Mrs. Miller." I left her at the fence and I joined my son and my wild animal in their innocent delights, and we got dirty and it was okay.

## 34

Night fell deep and dreamy, and Ronnie and I sat on our front porch, swinging gently in the hanging bench. It was one of those nights that felt textured like silk. I listened to the Nationals play terribly on the bluetooth speaker, and Ronnie's head rested on my shoulder as she drifted toward sleep.

She woke when her phone chimed. A text message, from Charlotte Andrews. She read it and passed the device to me.

Charlotte was apologizing to Ronnie for being a bitch. And to tell her she'd tried Ronnie's advice—she cooked dinner for her husband, a rarity, but she'd burned it, and she'd cleaned up the dishes but he'd been more surprised than thankful, and they had sex for the first time in weeks, and he'd gone to sleep afterward instead of locking up—so clearly Ronnie's advice was stupid but that was okay because so was her husband, lol, and she'd get a divorce from some other attorney and she hoped they could remain in touch.

I handed the phone back.

Ronnie said, "You cleaned the dishes tonight. And most nights. Was I grateful?"

"I don't remember," I said.

"I'll try to be."

"I don't do it so you'll be grateful."

"I know. But." She yawned. "I want to be a better wife than Charlotte is. Surely gratitude is part of that."

"Probably."

The screen door opened to admit Manny. He held a box in his hand. It took a lot to surprise Manuel Martinez, but he appeared to be.

"You know what these are?" He held the box for me to inspect—the set of red-tipped diamonds Marcus had given to me.

"Aurum," I said. "Criminal currency. So hot right now."

"You put the box on my bed?"

"I did," I said. "They're yours."

"Why?"

"Because I don't want them. Or, if I do, you're a good place to store them," I said.

"You don't understand their value."

"So I'm told."

"Looks like five are missing," he said.

"I spent five."

"*You* spent five aurum."

"I did," I said.

"On what?"

"Three arranging for Caleb and Robin to be smuggled into Mexico soon. One for the body of Ervin Lane to be destroyed. And one for the fake Caleb James report in Europe. You wouldn't believe the people Marcus knows," I said.

"You were hired to catch Caleb. But you messed up so bad, you had to spend five aurum to make him go away." Manny grinned.

"Too much?"

He waffled his hand. "Probably. Maybe. Who knows with these criminals." He closed the box with a snap. "Beck might know, actually. She's thick as thieves with them."

Ronnie smiled against my shoulder.

"That's funny. Noelle is thick as thieves," she said.

"Where'd you get the box?"

"Marcus. He suspects he'll be assassinated soon, and he wanted me to have them. He recorded the transfer in some ledger," I said.

Manny made a whistling sound.

"Did you already have some?" I said.

"A few."

"You ever spent any?"

He nodded. "Don't ask what for, *ese*. You won't like it."

"Now I wanna know so bad," I said.

A car drove by our lawn. Electric, barely made a whoosh, the lights punching holes in the dark.

"Who's gonna kill Marcus?" said Manny.

"Guy named Doyle."

Manny made a frown and scrubbed a hand through his hair. His gorgeous thick black hair. He needed a trim—some strands fell into his eyes.

"I know Doyle."

"Bad news?" I said.

"Not good news." He shook his head at the box of Aurum and everything it represented. "Ay, we shoulda stayed in Los Angeles. Safer there."

"I'm glad you didn't." Ronnie took my hand and squeezed it.

"That makes two of us, kid," I said.

Manny said we were gross and he went back inside, leaving us alone on the front porch.

Alone together.

THE END

❧

Dear Reader,

WHAT'S GOING on in my life, in 2022?

My wife and I celebrated our twenty-year anniversary, and we hope to sneak away for a week sometime this winter to someplace warm. We like each other and have a lunch date at least once a week, usually to our favorite Italian restaurant.

My first-born is a tenth grader and spends a lot of time at the gym. I enjoy watching him play soccer and he's involved with Young Life, and believes girls are mostly an irritation, even the prettier ones.

My second-born is an eighth grader who does his homework without being told to, and he has a hard time sleeping at night because he wants to talk, and recently he began beating me at board games, like Agricola. I'm not handling it gracefully.

My daughter continues to improve her English and math. She is the delight of her teachers, as well as her parents. She loves to eat noodles and watch YouTube and play with her friends outside.

Our dog Chloe sometimes limps for no reason, though it only lasts a few days. She's a Boston Terrier who makes shockingly good eye contact, and she is in love with the neighbor's German Shepherd.

We spent two weeks in the Outer Banks this summer and one week camping in North Carolina. (Glamping, really.)

I recently read *The Killer Angels*, by Shaara. It's a doozy, though I don't know if you'd like it if you're not into war or US history.

I highly recommend *Deep Work* by Newport if you're a

fiction writer or someone who wants to take a step forward in their career. And *I Hate the Ivy League* by Gladwell, if you're interested in colleges.

I've written twenty-eight books now (ten books for children, under a different name, and the rest are in the Mackenzie universe). I have the next three plotted in my mind already. (Book Two of the Atlanta Burning series, Book Five in the Sinatra series, and the first novel about Stackhouse, her origin story) Each working morning for the past eight years I sit at my computer and toil alone, inside my headphones, for four to six hours. It's solitary and it's difficult, but I *run* to work. I can't wait to do it again tomorrow. Because it means we'll be together again soon inside a good story.

Thank you for reading!


-ALAN


PS. If you haven't read The Wild South, it's time. Readers say it's the best book I've written. And I agree.

Made in the USA
Monee, IL
25 October 2022

16557160R00156